THAT
WAY AGAIN

THAT
WAY AGAIN

•

Carolyn Brown

AVALON BOOKS
NEW YORK

PRINTED IN THE UNITED STATES OF AMERICA
ON ACID-FREE PAPER
BY HADDON CRAFTSMEN, BLOOMSBURG, PENNSYLVANIA

To Charles
for all the reasons you know so well,
this one's for you

Chapter One

There wasn't a man on the face of the earth worth the bullet to put him six feet under. The only good ones were those with a tombstone marking their resting place, Bertha Mason thought that hot afternoon. Her back was rigid and the rocker barely moved. A soft, hot breeze blew across the porch and ruffled her thin, gray hair, but she didn't mind the stifling Oklahoma heat. Not that day, anyway. What she did mind was that boy, Preston Fleming. If only there was a way she could intervene between him and her great niece, Kitty Maguire, she'd do it. She'd sell her soul to the devil and dance a jig around a boiling pot of black witches just to see them break up, but her poor niece had too much of her own rapscallion Irish father in her to see things in the right perspective. Just like Timothy Maguire, Kitty thought with her heart instead of her mind. Kitty's mother hadn't listened to Bertha's warnings, and she'd proven Bertha right that time too.

1

Where the male gender was concerned Bertha was seldom, if ever, wrong.

Bertha picked up the cardboard fan from the table beside her chair. They didn't make fans like that anymore. Used to be every church had them right beside the hymnals in the wooden pockets on the back of the pews. The Lord's Prayer on one side in script lettering and the name of the local funeral home on the other. Seemed fitting. Shape up or ship out. No doubt, the boys made confetti out of them during the services and replacement costs were prohibitive. She sipped her ice cold lemonade and delicately fanned her wrinkled face.

She'd had icy lemonade on her wedding day, she remembered. She had gotten up that morning and her own dear mother had her white lawn wedding dress pressed and ready. There was lemonade on her breakfast tray along with thin pancakes that soaked up fresh sweet cream butter and pure maple syrup. Strange, she should recollect that day. Why, she hadn't thought of it in at least twenty years. It was best she didn't remember it often, especially since it was the day her heart had shattered. Looking back, though, she decided as she fanned herself, it had been for the best. That day might have been painful, but her eyes were opened where men were concerned. That was a lesson worth learning: A woman should always let her mind, not her heart, be the ruler. A heart was a deceitful thing made to steer a good woman wrong.

Preston Fleming wasn't any better than Jud Williams had been. Jud could have sent a note that morning but he didn't, and Bertha was left standing at the altar in her pretty white dress. She'd waited a whole hour before she'd given up and gone home with her parents. If only she could make Kitty understand. If Kitty would just listen to her and realize there wasn't anything but heartache around the corner. But the girl had that passionate Maguire blood in her veins. If Bertha could figure out a way to keep Kitty and Preston apart forever, she'd sure do it. Even if it meant giving up her front seat in heaven for one in the back forty acres of Hades on a barbed wire fence.

"Her mother shouldn't have died. She could make her see things right," Bertha mumbled. Kitty's mother had been the only grandchild on both sides of the family. Katherine Emily, Bertha's absolute joy. Katherine had been highly intelligent and shunned men just like Bertha had taught her. She'd gone to college. All the way to the top. Bertha thought her heart would explode with pride the day she sat in the audience and watched Katherine walk across the stage for her doctorate degree in architecture. Then that rotten Timothy Maguire came into her life. He weaseled his way into her heart and suddenly she was thinking with that instead of the brain the Good Lord gave her. Wasn't long until he convinced her to have a child, either, and now Bertha had this problem on her hands. It was all Timothy's fault. Men! Why couldn't God have made women capable of reproducing without them?

"Why couldn't Timothy have died instead of Katherine?" Bertha fumed. Her precious Katherine was diagnosed with an inoperable brain tumor when Kitty was just eleven years old. Just after the child's twelfth birthday, Katherine died. In her last words, she'd begged her ex-husband, Timothy, to let Bertha raise Kitty. Six years of hard work and it was all in vain. After a month of dating that Fleming boy, Kitty walked around with stars in her eyes, saying she was in love and they were getting married in a couple of years. Why, even at twenty the child wouldn't be able to think with the brain in her head. She'd let her heart rule her life and be miserable.

"Evenin'," Bertha's next-door-neighbor rounded the corner of the back porch and drew up the second rocker to sit a spell. "Think it might rain."

"Wish it would storm off somewhere in the ocean and a whole shipload of men would drown," Bertha snorted. "I wouldn't even be sorry to lose them all if Preston Fleming would just be gone."

"Ain't talked any sense into her yet?" Mable Smith asked.

"Thick-headed like her father." Bertha raised her chin and rolled her eyes.

"Well, out of sight, out of mind. She'll go off to that big school up in Tulsa tomorrow and mark my words, she will forget him. All those young fellows running around will take her eyes and heart away from that boy."

"I don't want that either. I want her to forget all of them. She needs to think about her schooling and being independent. Women don't need a man to be happy. I'm eighty years old and I've done all right," Bertha said.

Mable just nodded. Bertha had always been a strange sort. Ever since that rotten apple, Jud, disgraced her by leaving her at the altar. Never looked at another man after that. Just taught school until the school board made her retire and lived in the same house her parents had owned. She'd been a good friend all of Mable's life and an excellent neighbor. But Mable had learned years ago not to mention men folks around Bertha.

"Well, I just dropped by for a minute. Got bread raisin' so I'd better get on back home. Good luck. You still got one more day to talk sense into Kitty. You going to miss her bad?"

"Nope." Bertha shook her head. "Done all I could to raise the child proper. Took her to church with me. Fed her the right food. Made her go to bed on time. But miss her? Nope, can't say I will. Mostly I'll just be glad for the quietness. Eighty is too old to be worryin' about an eighteen-year-old."

"I'll run over tomorrow anyway. You make the lemonade and I'll bring some homemade bread and honey." Mable waved as she disappeared across the connecting backyards to her own little two bedroom frame house next door.

Bertha hauled herself up out of the rocking chair and opened the back door just as the phone rang. Her breath came in short gasps as she grabbed the receiver on the third ring. "Hello," she said, clutching her chest and taking a couple of deep breaths.

"Hello, Miss Bertha." Preston's deep voice made her cringe. "Is Kitty around? I've only got a few minutes. The line is long and there's lots of men folks wanting to call their loved ones."

"No, she's not here," Bertha said testily, then smiled as if an angel had just appeared at the back door. "But

she left a message for you. She said if you called I
was to tell you . . ."

"Oh," Preston sighed in disappointment. "Will she
be home in thirty minutes? That's about how long it'll
take me to make it through the line again. And we're
only supposed to talk three minutes. Didn't she get
my letter about when I was going to call?"

"Yes, she said you were supposed to call at five
today," Bertha said sweetly, the idea taking more and
more shape as she talked. The sharp twinge in her
chest subsided and she picked up the dishtowel to mop
the cold sweat from her forehead. Lying was a sin, but
surely God wouldn't lay it to her charge when it was
to protect Kitty.

"Is it five there?" Preston asked.

"It's four-thirty," Bertha told him.

"Well, I'll just go to the back of the line then,"
Preston said.

"No, don't. I said she'd left a message for you. Just
listen to me," she said sharply. "Kitty is going back
east to college. She's made lots of changes in her life
over the last week or two. I was sure she'd written
you all about it. There was a boy back there when she
went to visit her father for a few weeks in the summer.
Guess she's known him all these years. You know she
went two weeks every summer and a couple of weeks
at Christmas. Well, this boy has been calling every
day and she's decided to go back there for schooling
to be near him. She's fallen in love with him and
they're planning to marry at Christmas. She said to
tell you she'll send your little ring back to you and
for you not to bother writing any more."

"But . . ." Preston's voice cracked. Bertha could hear the pain and anguish even in just one word. Better that he know a little hurt than Kitty have to experience a lot of it later on down the road. She didn't feel one bit guilty.

"I guess your time is up, isn't it?" Bertha said.

"I suppose it is," Preston said. "Would you tell her that I still love her?"

"I don't think that's a wise thing right now," Bertha said. "She doesn't love you anymore. She doesn't need to hear that. Good-bye now, Preston. Next time you've got three minutes, call your mother." She hung up the phone.

Bertha had never told a lie in her entire life and was surprised that it had been so easy. Surely it was God's will, since it had just flowed from her mouth like pure truth. She could have danced a jig right there in the middle of the kitchen floor. Who said prayers didn't get answered? One minute she was fretting and the next the whole problem was solved. Well, at least half of it. The other half should be walking through the door any minute.

Kitty Maguire sang with the radio as she drove home from the Dairy Queen on the western side of Caddo, Oklahoma. She and her best friend, Lisa, had almost cried when they parted but Kitty promised she'd come back every weekend to help plan the wedding. After all, Kitty was the maid of honor and Lisa was too scatter-brained and in love with Jody to get the details in order. Lisa would get married at Christmas. And when Preston got out of the Navy, Lisa would be her matron of honor.

Everything was absolutely perfect.

Nothing could go wrong.

Not one single thing.

She'd been in love with Preston Fleming from the first minute she had seen him. It hadn't been easy, but they'd been wise enough to know that they couldn't get married as long as he was in the Navy. So she'd go on to college and at least get her first year finished before he got discharged. Then they'd finish the last three years together, and as partners of the Fleming Architectural Firm would set up business in Durant, Oklahoma.

"Aunt Bertha," she yelled at the front door. "Guess what? I heard on the radio that it's going to rain tomorrow. Can you believe it? All summer we've been praying for a storm cloud and the day I go off to college, they say it's going to rain."

"Preston called," Bertha said flatly, not even looking up from her knitting.

"Oh, I missed him." Kitty's voice registered disappointment. She sank down on the other end of the sofa from Bertha. "Is he going to call back? He said five, and I hurried so I'd be here. Did you tell him I'd be here at five?"

"I didn't tell him nothing. He did the talking," Bertha said. "He isn't calling back. Said he wouldn't have time. He gave me a message, though. Said to tell you that you could keep that little ring he gave you but he wouldn't be writing any more letters. Sit up straight, child. Don't slump."

"He said what?" Kitty's throat constricted and she couldn't swallow past the lump. Aunt Bertha never played jokes.

"He said there was another woman. One of those Navy women he'd met and they were going to get married soon as he got to California. Said that he was sorry if you were upset with him, but he was really in love with this other lady. I guess he wanted to get married bad, and when you wanted to go on to school, it didn't set too well with him. Guess some men just want a wife no matter what," she said matter-of-factly.

"But I love him," Kitty whispered. "He said he loved me. He didn't mention another woman." The room began to spin and her head was a tunnel with an echo on one end and a throbbing ache on the other.

"I've been telling you," Bertha pointed a knitting needle at her, "for three months that you don't need a man to make you happy. I've been telling you he'd just hurt you. And I was right, wasn't I? Now dry your eyes and go get your things ready. Bedtime will be here soon and you need to get to your packing."

"But Aunt Bertha, he said he loved me as deep as the Red River runs." Tears flowed down Kitty's face and dripped off her chin onto her white T-shirt.

"The Red River isn't anything but a stream in the summertime so he didn't love you that much, did he?"

"I love him so much." She bent over until her head lay on the arm of the sofa and wept. Her chest hurt so bad she could scarcely breath, so the sobs came out in ragged gasps.

"No you don't. You don't even know what love is at eighteen. No woman does. Now go finish your packing. You've got your whole life ahead of you, girl. Don't lay there acting like a baby."

Kitty made her weak knees carry her to her bedroom, but that's as far as they could go before she collapsed. She buried her face in the big brown teddy bear Preston won for her at the carnival and sobbed quietly so that Aunt Bertha couldn't hear. Her perfect world was shattered into a million jagged pieces, but there was no way a person could ever count how many pieces her heart had broken into. How could Preston treat her like that? Just yesterday she had received a letter from him reassuring her of his undying love. A love that would always be as deep as the river ran in the spring when the rains fell.

She finally picked up her stationary and began to write. If he could just understand how much she loved him, maybe he wouldn't marry that other woman. Tears dotted the letter as she wrote, begging him to reconsider. *Please, please call Aunt Bertha as soon as you can. I will leave my number at the dorm room. Oh, my darling, Preston, don't do this to us. I love you so much. If you want to get married now, I can go to school in California. Plans can be changed even in the middle of a semester. Please call me or write me.* The letter went on for ten pages, each word twisting her heart into a pretzel.

She slipped it into the envelope and put two heart stickers on the outside, just like she always did. Then she finished her packing. The next morning, after a totally sleepless night, she stood the teddy bear up in the middle of her bed. "I can't take you with me, Bear. Too many memories," she said in a cracked voice.

"Keep this for me, Bear. If he calls, I'll put it back on next week." She took her ring off, put it on a gold chain, then looped it around the bear's neck.

Bertha whistled as she bustled around in the kitchen. Should she make oatmeal for Kitty before she left or French toast? The child scarcely ate breakfast but she'd need something in her stomach. Tulsa was a long drive.

"Don't cook for me, Aunt Bertha," Kitty said from the living room. "I'm not hungry. I'm going to load my things into the truck and get on down the road. I want to be there before lunchtime. I want to meet my roommate and get things settled. There's some kind of freshman to-do tonight and classes start tomorrow."

"Well, you drive careful now, child. Don't go over the speed limit." Bertha nodded but didn't make an effort to hug her niece. She had discouraged such things from the beginning. Hugging just made a child dependent, and Bertha had been determined to put a backbone of steel in Kitty.

"I will. I'll call as soon as I get there with my phone number. If Preston calls back, please give it to him." Kitty choked when she said his name.

"He won't be calling back," Bertha said. "Study hard now and make something out of yourself."

"Okay." Kitty nodded. "You've got the address. If there's any mail for me just forward it."

"Your dad only writes once a week and you've already given him the address. I heard you telling him on the phone when said you made up your mind to take his offer and go to school in Tulsa rather than Durant."

"Well, this is it, then. I guess I'll see you next weekend."

Kitty longed to hug her aunt. She'd learned early that Bertha wasn't the loving type back when she was twelve. Kitty had only been in the house a couple of days and had had a terrible nightmare one night. She sobbed all the way down the hall into Aunt Bertha's room. The lecture she got that night taught her to keep her fears to herself.

"I'll be here. You might change your mind once you get up there and start having a good time. Don't bother calling if you aren't coming, though. Those long distance calls cost too much. If you don't show up, I'll know you changed your mind," Bertha said. "Better get your things in the truck. Clouds are gathering. Looks like the weather man was right."

The first drops fell just as Kitty backed out of the driveway. Gray skies. A slow drizzling rain. Just like in her heart. She'd once read part of a poem that said that tears on the outside fall to the ground and are slowly washed away, but tears on the inside fall on the soul and stay and stay and stay. She wondered if the tears on her soul would ever disappear.

Bertha ate her oatmeal slowly. She read the morning paper while she finished her tea. Kitty had been gone an hour. If she'd forgotten anything, she would have been back long before now. So it was safe. Her bones creaked when she stood up, but she felt better than she had in months. Three months to be exact. So what if it took two little white lies to take care of the matter. In the end it saved Kitty a lot of heartache.

She opened the front door. The smell of rain,

cleansing the world as it fell slowly, filled her nostrils. She sucked in another lung full. It was an omen. God was giving her a sign she'd done the right thing. She'd flushed that worthless man right out of Kitty's life. Bertha went to the mailbox and removed the letter pinned there for the mailman to take when he arrived at mid-morning. Two heart stickers on the back and Preston's military address on the front. A couple of small water stains. Either Kitty's tears or raindrops. She hoped it was raindrops and that Kitty had written him a scorching letter of anger.

But she wouldn't open it. No sir. That wouldn't be right. Reading someone else's mail would be downright dishonest. She hustled down the hallway into her bedroom and hid the letter in an old manila envelope she'd gotten years ago from Katherine. It had held pictures of Kitty when she was a little girl. When a week had passed without another letter arriving, she would burn them. One by one. A little fire in the old burning barrel down at the end of the lot. She slipped the aged, yellow envelope beneath the sweaters in her bottom dresser drawer.

Phone calls? She'd just repeat her story, which was becoming more real with every moment.

Chapter Two

Kitty parked the truck in the driveway and stared at the house for a full five minutes. Nothing had changed. Not in five years. It didn't even need painting. She took a deep breath and made herself get out of the vehicle. She should have hired someone to do the job. Surely there was a private firm somewhere that took care of liquidations when people didn't want houses anymore. But she'd studied enough psychology to know that this would bring closure, and Kitty felt a desperate need for that. Then she could put the whole ordeal of the past behind her. Maybe even date and fall in love again.

"Yeah, right." Kitty sighed as she slung open the door of the light blue Chevrolet truck. "I won't ever feel that way again. I just know it in my bones."

The dead brown grass crunched under her feet as she crossed the lawn but she scarcely noticed. Her heart skipped a beat, then took off so fast she could

14

scarcely breathe. She couldn't go back into that house where she'd known so much pain, but she couldn't stay out of it, either. She had to open the door, walk in, make decisions, stay a week and then leave Caddo forever.

She pulled the key from the pocket of her purse with shaking hands. It was silly. It was just a house. A plain little two bedroom frame house in a small town in southern Oklahoma. The house where she'd lived after she was twelve years old. Where she'd lived when she met Preston . . . she wouldn't go there. Not today. *Not right now*, she told herself. She'd face that dragon later. Today's toad frog would be to walk through the house and make decisions about what, if anything, she wanted to keep.

"Toad frog," she whispered with an almost-smile, remembering her father telling her that she should get up every morning and eat a live toad frog. Anything else the day could throw at her would be nothing compared to that. Well, today her toad frog was simply to enter the house and not hyperventilate.

She took a deep breath and kicked the door open with her toe. The door squeaked. Aunt Bertha would have had the oil can out greasing the hinges if she'd heard it. Kitty set her suitcase and a portable CD player on the floor beside the sofa. Stiffly starched antimacassars were pinned to the back of the sofa and the easy chairs. Doilies were on every table in the room. She could see the reflection of her mint-green walking shorts in the glow of the oak hardwood floors. It looked just like it had the day she walked out of it on her way to college, taking most of her belongings along with her broken heart.

She stood in the middle of the floor, looking at the inside of the house that had never changed from the time she was a small child and had come there with her mother. If a murder had been committed in this house, she would methodically go over every detail and use the clues to help create a profile of the perpetrator. That was her job. Pure, simple clues to find the person who'd broken the law. However minute, there were always clues. It had nothing to do with a fickle heart or emotions of any kind. Just plain signs and working up a psychological profile as to what that person was thinking or not thinking when he had committed the crime. Kitty's heart and soul had died in this house one fine August day, five years before, but she didn't need to check to see if any pictures on the wall were askew in the fight, nor did she need to look at a dead body on the floor, or gather bits of evidence from the crime scene. She knew who the perp was, and he'd gotten off without even a slap on the wrist from the local judge.

Mable Smith had kept her end of the bargain. Kitty had mailed her a check once a month and she'd taken care of the property. Could it really have been only five years? To Kitty it had been eons since her heart had stopped functioning and since she'd tried so desperately to stop grieving for what could not be. She sucked up a lung full of stale air and went down the short hallway to her old bedroom. It was exactly the same as that morning when she'd left Caddo. The teddy bear kept a silent sentinel in the middle of the bed. The chain holding the ring with a small diamond in an open heart still hung around his neck. He was still protecting a futile future for her. She should have thrown away the bear and tossed the ring in the toilet. But she'd stroked his brown fur so often, read him so many letters, sobbed with him so many nights out of loneliness, that she couldn't think of throwing him away. Instead of burning or trashing him, she'd sentenced him to five years of solitary confinement.

The ring was a different matter. She didn't know if she'd ever be able to throw it away. Kitty hugged herself against a cold blast of air from the ceiling vent. The night Preston Fleming put that ring on her finger a hot rush had filled her body. Nothing could go wrong from that day forward. They were ready to face the world together—that night.

Memories that she didn't want to surface swirled around her in a kaleidoscope of colors. Blue, like her heart, Preston's eyes, and the pickup truck he'd helped her choose just before he went back to Philadelphia. The one she still drove because every time she thought she was ready to trade it in, she couldn't. Yellow, like the sparkling sunshine reflected in his eyes the day they played like kindergartners at the Caddo park. Red, like the heart stickers they sealed all their letters with. Two hearts. One for Preston. One for her. Stuck so that they overlapped. Her knees started to buckle, so she sat down on the stool in front of her kidney-shaped vanity with a yellow-checked skirt.

There was the same old Kitty Maguire staring back at her from a smudge-free mirror. The same chestnut brown hair. The brown from her mother, the Mason side of her gene pool, and red highlights from her father, Timothy Maguire. Light gray eyes from her paternal grandmother, which looked totally out of place with the rest of her Irish features. The same grandmother had provided the genes for her peaches-and-cream complexion arriving in the wrong century. Older women swooned with envy when they saw her smooth, buttermilk-white skin. Young girls pitied her because she could not tan. A dimple on the left side when she smiled came from her mother. A Kitty Maguire identical to the one who had walked out of the room, except the eyes didn't look young anymore. They didn't sparkle like they had when she was eighteen and had the naiveté to actually believe what people said.

"I had it once but I won't ever feel that way again," she whispered to the young woman in the mirror. "Some people never even get it the first time. Once is a miracle. Twice is an impossibility. I'm not so sure it's the right thing anyway. Not anymore." To be led around by the passions of the heart could get a woman in more trouble than she could wiggle out of.

She tried to shake off a sense of pure dread. The front door squeaked open, and she jumped away from the image in the mirror. Then she relaxed when she heard Mable's thin, wispy voice floating down the hallway.

"Miss Kitty. Miss Kitty, are you in here?" Mable asked.

"I'll be right out," Kitty called back. She shut her eyes, put away the past and pasted on a smile. Even if it was fake, Mable wouldn't notice. Few people did.

"I peeked out the window and saw your truck." Mable smiled when Kitty entered the living room.

"Everything looks wonderful," Kitty said. Mable's hair was even whiter than it had been and was so wispy it barely covered her pink scalp. She didn't stand ramrod straight anymore, either. Aunt Bertha would fuss and fume about Mable's terrible posture if she was still around.

"Thank you." The woman beamed. "I kept it just like it was the day I found our dear Bertha in the rocking chair on the back porch. Just sitting there like she did every morning. Such a shock. I'm sure you've grieved for her, seeing as how she was so close to you. I've got to admit, I'm glad you're getting rid of the house though. I've decided to move to Arizona with my son. These old bones just get worse and worse and it's time for me to give up housekeeping. Had an auction last week. We'll be moving in a day or so now."

"Neighborhood sure is changing," Kitty commented.

"Yes, it will. Probably young folks will buy up these two houses. Hope they take care of them. My folks and Bertha's built them close together because our mothers were such good friends. You still got that truck, I see." Mable nodded toward the front door. "I figured you would have traded it in a long time ago. When you got your degree. What was it you decided to do? Be one of them fancy-schmancy people who make up house plans like Preston Fleming?"

"No," Kitty said, blushing slightly at even hearing his name spoken aloud. "I'm a profiler for the FBI."

"Oh, so you're a policeman. Seems a strange job for a woman and all. Women in my day might've worked like your dear aunt at teaching school, or maybe were nurses, but they weren't policemen. Reckoned I'd see you driving up here in one of them fancy sports cars," she said bluntly.

"I thought about trading it in," Kitty said. "I might after the auction. I'm not a policeman. I work for the FBI. It's a different line of work. I need to write you a final check for this last month." Kitty pulled her checkbook from the purse she'd tossed on the sofa and went to the little desk in the corner to write out the amount. "You can't begin to know how much I appreciate all you've done, Mrs. Smith. I knew you'd be taking care of everything so I didn't worry about it one bit."

"Thank you." Mable slipped the check into her apron pocket. "I was glad to do it. It's all working out just fine. FBI, huh? Well, it's all police work to me. Do they let you drive one of them black and white cars with a siren on top?"

"No, ma'am. Just that truck out there," Kitty said.

"Well, don't you worry none, honey. If you work hard, maybe in a few years they'll give you one of them cars so you can stop people who speed through town and give them a ticket. We could sure use you right here in Caddo. Young people zip down these roads so fast it's a sin. Well, I've got to get back. Packing, you know. It's quite a job, but I want to go through everything myself and not toss out anything I might want later. You've got the same thing to do. It won't be easy going through your dear aunt's things.

Never is. Let me know if you need anything. I washed your sheets and remade your bed so it's all clean. Didn't know what you wanted or I would have put some things in the ice box for you."

"That's quite all right. I'll probably eat out most of the time anyway." She followed Mable to the door.

"Good luck with this job and just keep at it. You'll work your way up to one of them cars if you do good." Mable stopped and looked around the house one more time.

"Thanks," Kitty said. A smile twitched at the corners of her mouth and her gray eyes almost sparkled. "Well, time to go to work and quit reminiscing," she scolded herself. "I'll have to ask Jasper if I can have a black and white car when I get back to Oklahoma City." She picked up her suitcase and carried it to her bedroom where she flipped it on the bed. She took out two dresses fit for Sunday morning mass, several faded, worn T-shirts, a few pairs of shorts and one nice chambray jumper. That would get her through the week.

She patted the bear on her way out of the room, but no shivers chased down her spine. Maybe it wasn't going to be so hard after all. She'd just worked the whole ordeal up to be a mountain when it could barely be classified as a molehill. That's what happened when the heart ruled the body instead of the brain.

The refrigerator had been plugged in and was cool, but it was as bare as Mother Hubbard's cupboard. She'd purchase fruit, cheese, a few cans of soup, pretzels and coffee. The house was spotless so she didn't need cleaning supplies. Her stomach growled louder than the motor of the ancient refrigerator. She'd left Tulsa early that morning and hadn't taken time to eat breakfast. Suddenly, the black cloud that had hovered over her since she'd decided to sell the whole kit and caboodle was gone, and she was hungry. She wanted a big double bacon cheeseburger with fries and even a chocolate malt from the Dairy Queen out east of town.

"And be hanged to the calories," she said as she grabbed her purse and pulled the door shut behind her. "I'm so hungry I could eat a bear." She smiled and the slight dimple in her left cheek deepened. She crossed the bridge with the arch welcoming everyone to Caddo, Oklahoma and telling them the town was founded in 1872. Surprisingly, it continued to go right on existing all these years. The population of 916 never changed much. One elderly fellow at church once said that every now and then a girl came up in the family way and some old boy high tailed it out of town, and that kept the population pretty close to the same number. She hadn't thought of that man in years and was still trying to remember his name when she nosed her truck into a parking place beside the front door of the Dairy Queen.

The place was empty except for two elderly women licking ice cream cones in the booth behind her and discussing the upcoming auction between slurps. "Well, it's about time she took care of that house. Poor old Mable Smith can't go on cleaning it forever, you know, even if the money is good. Girl must be richer than Midas to pay that much just to do a little dusting and chase a mop over the floors once a week. I heard

Mable is going to Arizona with her son real soon. I went to her auction last week. Picked up the cutest little magazine rack. Real oak. Wouldn't Bertha Mason just die if she knew all her pretty things were going to be auctioned off? I tell you one thing, I'm going to be the first one there. I want those crocheted pieces for my house. And I've coveted those little cherry end tables in her living room forever. They go all the way back to her parents' time. Course she was born and died right there in that house so I guess they would. They're real antiques, you know. Not those pieces of junk you find these days in the so-called antique shops," one lady said.

"Well, I'm going to be right beside you. I never seen the stuff but you can point out the good things. I heard that Kitty Maguire was a real handful for Bertha to raise. I bet it was just too much on her old heart," one whispered to the other. "I never met the girl myself but I've heard some pretty ugly things went on just before she ran back east to that high faultin' college and Bertha dropped dead a few days later. Don't know why she had to go there with a good school right over in Durant. Guess Bertha's way of livin' wasn't good enough for her once she finished high school and could run away."

"Well, I wouldn't know the girl. Only ever saw her once and that was at graduation that year. Great granddaughter graduated with her. Must be five years ago now. Knew Bertha all my life. She was a strange bird but honest as the day was long."

They leaned their heads together and whispered and Kitty wondered just what she'd been so ugly about.

Mercy, she'd gone to Tulsa to college one week, Aunt Bertha died the next and she'd never come back. Not even for the funeral. She had a week of classes, and on Saturday morning when she was supposed to come home to help Lisa plan the wedding, she had awakened with severe stomach pains. Her roommate rushed her to the hospital where they diagnosed her with acute appendicitis. What should have been an overnight stay turned into a week when there were complications with the surgery. Her father called every day, but then one morning there he was standing beside her bed when she opened her eyes.

"Daddy, you didn't have to come here," she'd said, but secretly was elated to see him.

"Mrs. Smith found your Aunt Bertha dead this morning. She had a heart attack while sitting in her rocker. She found your number and called the school. Chain of command found my number on your enrollment card so here I am. I'll go make the arrangements." He hugged her gently.

Bertha was blood kin and Kitty ought to shed tears for her, but she couldn't. The fact that she couldn't even cry for the aunt who'd kept her six years bothered Kitty to distraction. She stared through the picture on the hospital wall all day trying to remember good things that she would miss and wondering if her heart was so permanently scarred by Preston that she would never feel anything again.

Timothy Maguire hired a private plane to take him to Caddo where he made all the funeral arrangements in less than an hour. Then he went back to Tulsa to spend the evening with Kitty before boarding a jet to fly back to his own job with the FBI.

"I should cry," Kitty told her father that evening. "It's not right that there isn't sadness in my heart."

"Your Aunt Bertha was a strange woman. Your mother told me a few things about her while we were married. Aunt Bertha was a good woman. Upstanding citizen of that little town. Schoolteacher and all. But she got left at the altar when she was a young woman and it warped her mind where men were concerned. Never liked them after that. Not any of them, and especially not me." Timothy chuckled. "Her heart grew a layer of stone around it. Don't ever let that happen to you, my child."

"I won't, Daddy," she said.

"Oh, by the way, everything she owned is in that house and she's left it all to you. I thought you might like to call that neighbor of hers, Mable Smith, to keep an eye on things. Offer her a nice bit of money each month and you can worry with what do with it later."

Now, five years later, sitting there listening to the women discuss her lack of virtues, Kitty remembered that conversation. Was it because she didn't cry when Aunt Bertha died that made her ugly? If so, how did these women know that?

Kitty had been a model student and child. Valedictorian of her senior class. Student council president. Cheerleader. She sang in the choir at Aunt Bertha's church on Sunday. Never got into trouble or came home late. Not one thing for Aunt Bertha to complain to Timothy about when he picked Kitty up for holidays or visited when he could.

She pushed the last half of her cheeseburger away. It smelled horrid and the malt was just something cold and wet. An undercurrent of ill will chilled her to the bone.

Caddo had a small grocery store, but she didn't want any more citizens of Caddo staring at her and making snide remarks behind her back. She needed a few supplies to last the week so she made up her mind in that instant to drive down to Durant, to one of the big supermarkets where no one would recognize her. She drove down the two lane highway through the tiny little berg of Armstrong and back south into Durant. When she checked her speedometer she was going ninety miles an hour. *Oh, well,* she sighed but she didn't take her foot off the gas. Jasper always fussed at her speeding. Told her that she drove too fast to try to get away from her haunted past. She checked the rearview mirror. No highway patrolmen. No ominous black clouds hanging on the horizon. Just a hot, southern Oklahoma summer day. She drove fast because she liked the speed. It had nothing to do with the past, haunted or otherwise.

She sang with the radio at the top of her lungs, but instead of the noise obliterating every thought of Preston, the song brought memories of him right into the truck with her. His dark hair in a military cut. The way his baby blue eyes smoldered when they looked down at her. The happiness they'd shared the night he won the bear.

She wasn't going to think about him. She would erase the memory with another one. One of her mother before she got sick. Maybe the day they went to the park, had a picnic and fed the ducks, but that brought back memories of going to the park in Caddo with Preston—the day he slid down the slide with her in front of him, his arms wrapped tightly around her and the warmth of his breath on her neck. The slight cleft in his chin that quivered when he chuckled. The way her crazy heart hurt when he drove away that night.

She shook off that image and thought about the day her father brought her from Tulsa to Caddo to live with her Aunt Bertha, but that caused her to remember the day Bertha told her about the phone call. Finally, when she passed Chief Road leading back to the Fleming farm, she gave up trying, and let it all come back with a rush. Might as well face it, try to flush it out of her heart, and then get on with life. She'd known she couldn't run from it forever, and apparently today was the day it was going to surface, whether she wanted to or not. Five years worth of painful, dirty laundry hidden away in the back of her mind.

Usually Preston drove home from Durant through Kenefic to his ranch. The road was better if he went through Caddo but he hated driving past the Mason house even after five years. Just a quick glimpse of that little white frame house still squeezed his heart with an incurable ache. But he'd had supper at his folks' house, so he had to drive home through Caddo or go fifteen miles out of the way. He wasn't about to admit that someone as fickle as Kitty Maguire could still hold sway over his heart.

He'd eaten too much, but then he always did when he had supper at the Fleming farm with his parents and all his siblings. He moaned and patted his stomach, promising himself that after a long, cool shower he would sit on his deck and watch the sunset, smell the fresh air and listen to the birds sing before they went to roost—and not touch a single bite of food before breakfast. Not even a handful of pretzels or a bowl of ice cream.

He loved the solitude of his small ranch. The quietness, the lack of city noises, and especially the sunrises and sunsets. It was the nice part of owning his own firm: designing houses for woody lots or rocky hillsides. He made a lot of money. That entitled him to as much property as he wanted to own and he could be a hermit if he wanted.

Alan Jackson's song, "Where Were You When the World Stopped Turning," came on the radio. Preston applied the song to his own heart. Where was he when the world stopped turning five years ago? Standing with a telephone to his ear, with a long line of military men behind him.

He didn't want to think about that. He'd shake it off and call Tammy when he got home; ask her to come over and watch the sunset with him. They'd had a standing date for Friday night for the past six months. Dinner, movies and back to her house . . . sometimes for a quick peck on the cheek as she yawned and got out of the car, sometimes a lingering kiss, but nothing very exciting, to be honest. Certainly nothing as exciting as Kitty Maguire had been all those years ago, but he was stupid back in those days. Since then he'd guarded his heart and soul as defensively as he had protected his country when he was in the Navy.

"I won't ever feel that way again," he reassured himself aloud. "It was too intense, too deep anyway. Besides, finding another woman like Kitty to make me feel that way again would be nothing short of a miracle. I'll just call Tammy and get her off my mind. No I won't! Forget asking Tammy over," he mumbled, angry with himself for even saying Kitty's name. "Wednesday. Choir practice night, and far be it for her to miss church. Oh well, a long evening on the porch and . . . *what is that*?" He stomped on the brakes, leaving twenty feet of skid marks on the highway. He looked into the rearview mirror, and sure enough it was there. His mother's wonderful cooking had not provoked an hallucination. That really was Kitty Maguire's truck sitting in the driveway. Five long years and out of the clear blue summer sky she decided to come back to Caddo. Had she brought her Yankee husband with her, he wondered?

"Kitty," he said hoarsely, wishing he could forget her name, her face, those deep auburn highlights in her hair sparkling in the blistering hot afternoon sun. He didn't need to close his eyes to see the tears welling up in her gray eyes that final day when he kissed her good-bye. Or to see the way she stood at the back of that little blue truck and waved until she couldn't see his car anymore.

He remembered the passion in her letters, even the last one when she was two-timing him with that other man. Suddenly, he wondered what she'd done with the teddy bear, the one he gave her on their first date. Or the little ring with the open heart.

"Probably burned it along with all my letters when she went off east and married that fellow." He pulled off the road. He got out of his truck and watched the house, as if the blue truck might disappear in a vapor of smoke. He should drive right up and knock on the door. When she opened it he should ask her if she was happy with her decision to dump him without any kind of explanation other than the message she left with her Aunt Bertha; if she'd paid for the day she wrecked his whole world and left his heart in a puddle of tears in Trinidad.

He remembered the excitement building up in him as he had waited in line to use the telephone. Three minutes, no more, was all he could talk, but to hear her voice would be enough. To know that she still loved him as much as she said in her letters. The first time he had seen her gray eyes twinkling in the afternoon sun, he'd known she was the girl he would marry.

Preston was heartsick all over again as he remembered the conversation with Bertha word for word. He continued to stare out the rearview window of his own gray Dodge truck at the blue Chevrolet. The truck he had helped her choose. Blue to match his eyes and remind her of him every time she looked at it, she'd said that day at the dealership. She'd used her mother's life insurance money to buy it. At least part of the policy allowed for that after she graduated from high school. The rest was in a trust fund to be used for her college expenses. Wherever she wanted to go.

However long it took. Then there was a big sum to be given to her the day she got her degree, with the balance to be hers when she was twenty-five.

It was all laid down on paper. Just like their lives were laid down in the depths of their hearts. But she'd ruined it all when she tossed what they had out the window for some Yankee who had been in love with her when she was all of twelve years old. Well, he hoped she had awakened one fine morning and all she could think of was Preston Fleming and the way her heart did double time when he held her in his arms.

He hoped she was as miserable as he was.

Chapter Three

Listening to country singer Sara Evans's CD wasn't what her father, Timothy, would have prescribed for Kitty that evening when she donned her cut off jean shorts and a faded T-shirt and commenced sorting through everything in the house. Country music was made to make a person sad, he had said repeatedly, whereas Celtic music stirred the happiness in their souls. Sara sang about looking into those blue eyes and something happening to her, but all she'd hear tonight would be true lies. Kitty wondered if Sara Evans had ever met Preston Fleming.

She methodically filled several pages in a notebook concerning what she wanted to keep and what she would toss out in the auction. This was something she understood: notes, systematic decisions, routines was the only thing that made a bit of sense. When she made up her mind to have the auction and sell the house, she'd promised herself that she would only haul back to her apartment as much as she could load in the back of her pickup truck. Her apartment could scarcely accommodate extra furniture, but some of the pieces were heirlooms.

On the CD player, Sara began singing a song about an unopened letter. One of the lines said something about a love that is trust without reason, and Kitty's mind went again to Preston. He had promised to love her, but he sure hadn't stood up too well when he got out on the high seas.

"You might be right, Daddy," she mumbled as she carried the teddy bear to the living room and set him on the sofa. Then she shook her head and took him back to the bedroom. "I probably do need to listen to classical music like Momma or Celtic like you, because everything I touch, taste, smell or even hear reminds me of Preston." She hugged the bear and put him back on the bed. She'd take him and the ring back to her apartment and decide what to do with them later—after the auction and when she'd left Caddo for the last time.

"Of course, I'm right," she heard her father's voice as surely as if it were in the room with her. "Celtic music is what you need. A bit of the old 'Danny Boy,' or 'Ramblin' Irishman.' "

"Well, I like country," Kitty argued. "Even if it does remind me of Preston." She slid open the bottom drawer of the dresser in her old room.

There they were. A whole line of letters from Preston. Untouched for many years. She ran her forefinger over the envelopes. She wouldn't read them. Not a single one. She'd throw them out.

"Miss Kitty?" The door squeaked and she heard Mable's voice at the same time.

"Back here," she yelled. "In my bedroom."

"Miss Kitty, my son is here. I wanted to say good-bye. We'll be leaving early tomorrow mornin' and all. Oh my, child you haven't even started yet." She looked at Kitty sitting on the floor with a drawer pulled out. "You better get busy." She shook her finger under Kitty's nose.

"Yes, ma'am, I guess I better. Mrs. Smith, did you know I was in the hospital when they buried Aunt Bertha?"

"Nope, didn't know why you didn't come to the funeral. Some fellow flew down here and planned it all right nice. Heard tell at the time it was Bertha's nephew or something like that. We never even knew she had a nephew." Maple screwed her face up into a thousand extra wrinkles as she tried to remember that far back. "Oh, I recollect now, it was that man that married Katherine. He came and took care of things. I figured I'd see you there. Seemed strange, but then kids are unpredictable at that age, and there was that business about the Fleming boy and the other one. Miss Bertha was going to explain it all to me, she said. I never did understand all that went on when you left. Miss Bertha was sitting on the porch the day before you left and we talked about that Fleming boy. Then Bertha up and died. Did you know that I found her on the back porch? She looked just like she always did except her eyes were shut. Well, funny how it all worked out, ain't it? You come back to Caddo and

I'm leaving. I'm glad to be moving. It ain't been the same without Bertha. I'll be going now. Good-bye and get busy, child."

"Yes, ma'am," Kitty nodded. "Good luck to you."

"You too. And you just stay with that police job. Some day they might just give you one of them cars. Kids these days hop from one job to another and never stick with what they got. You make your Aunt Bertha proud of you even if she has gone on to heaven," she said, her finger waggling at Kitty.

"Yes, ma'am." Kitty watched Mable shuffle out the door.

"Mercy, does age do that to all women? And why was I such a pack rat?" she asked herself, shifting from one thought to the other without a pause. She shut the drawer with the letters and opened another one. "I've got seven days and nights to think about those silly letters. I won't think about them today. Just like Scarlett in *Gone With The Wind*, I shall put off until tomorrow that which is distasteful today." She threw the back of her hand across her forehead and intoned dramatically, but even that didn't bring a hint of a grin to her face.

Kitty pushed the door open in the Wal-Mart and saw the pay telephone. She'd really meant to call Lisa the day before, but she completely forgot when she overheard the conversation in the Dairy Queen. Surely Lisa had grown up in the past five years and gotten over whatever snit she'd been in when Kitty had phoned her after the hospital stay. Now that had been a pure puzzle. When she got back to her dorm room after the surgery she'd called Lisa, who'd acted like some possessed woman rather than her faithful friend of six years. She'd told Kitty she would never forgive her for what she'd done, and then threw in something about not attending her dear little old aunt's funeral. Before Kitty could get a word in edgewise, Lisa hung up on her. Kitty gave her friend a couple of days to cool off and tried to call again. Her mother informed her that Lisa wasn't home and never to call there again. A week later she sat down and wrote Lisa a long letter begging her to tell her what she'd done that wouldn't warrant forgiveness. She told her about the horrid experience she'd had with the surgery and explained that was the reason she couldn't attend the funeral. She asked her to please call and they'd talk. She'd tried to tell Lisa about the problem with Preston, but she couldn't make herself write his name.

Lisa never answered the letter or called.

At the time, it just seemed to be another incident in a long string of bad luck. But now that she was in Caddo, Kitty felt a need deep in her heart to find out just what had set her best friend off. They weren't teenagers anymore. Surely they could sit down and discuss the problem. She fished around in her purse for a couple of quarters and plugged them into the slot. She punched in Lisa's home number, glad she could at least remember it from her high school days.

Lisa didn't know about Kitty's life in college. She didn't know about the safe little rut Kitty lived in. One where she went to school, studied until her eyes wouldn't stay open and then dreamed of Preston every night. Slowly, she built a wall around herself, refusing to let friends inside. The only people she really trusted were her father and her boss, Jasper.

"Hello," Lisa's mother answered the phone.

"Hi, Pat, this is Kitty Maguire. I'm trying to get in touch with Lisa." The silence was deafening.

"Why?" Icicles hung on the edges of the single word.

"I'm back in town to have an auction. Aunt Bertha's house and everything. I just wanted to visit with Lisa while I was here. Figure out what went wrong with our friendship all those years ago," Kitty said, that same cold feeling of an ill wind traveling down her spine that she'd felt in the Dairy Queen the day before.

"I see. Well, I don't know if she'll talk to you, but that's her decision," Lisa's mother snipped. "She and Jody live in Durant. The number's in the book so you can look it up. I'm not about to give it to you. I'd have to listen to her ranting and raving if I did. Good-bye."

"Whew!" Kitty exhaled loudly and picked up the phone book hanging by a chain beside the phone. Fortunately the page with Lisa's number hadn't been ripped out and she dialed the number and waited.

"Hello Lisa?" Kitty smiled when she recognized the familiar voice of her old friend.

"Yes, that's me," she said.

"This is Kitty Maguire. I'm in town for an auction to take care of Aunt Bertha's property and I . . ."

Another long, pregnant silence.

"Lisa, are you there?"

"Yes, I am, Kitty, but don't call here again. I told you I never wanted to hear from you after what you did. You *were* my friend but so was Preston. You didn't even have the good grace to write him and tell him. So don't be calling here and expecting me to still be your friend. Poor old Preston is just now getting back to normal. I don't want to talk to you," she said coldly.

"Wait a minute," Kitty stormed. What was Lisa talking about anyway? What she did to poor Preston? Kitty suffered a broken heart and now it was poor *Preston*?

"No, you wait a minute." Lisa's tone rose an octave. "You're the one who did him dirty then ran away, so don't expect me to come crawling back into our friendship. Just go on back east with your rich Yankee husband. I can't believe you were such an actress, not even telling me that last day we were together. I thought we were friends. Then you run off to the east, not to Tulsa where you told me you were going."

"What are you talking about? Back east? A husband? I wrote you," Kitty said.

"Yeah, right. A letter wanting me to explain what you already knew. Like you didn't understand. For crying out loud, Kitty, I wasn't stupid. If it hadn't been for Jody, poor Preston would have lost his mind."

Kitty heard the hard click and held the receiver out from her ear for a while before she finally put it back on the hook. Something was severely wrong with the picture Lisa had painted. What was that about a rich Yankee husband?

Kitty threw her purse in the cart and frowned as she tried to figure out what on earth had been said when she left town all those years ago. She absentmindedly pushed the cart around the aisles while she tried to make sense of the whole thing. Lisa's main concern had been poor Preston. Well, what about poor Kitty?

"Poor old, tired Kitty," she mumbled. She'd worked hard half the night, collapsing on her bed at three o'clock in the morning, but at least that room was finished. All except the one drawer where the letters were. When she had awakened at noon, she wanted pizza. Real pizza with extra cheese and pepperoni. Not one of those frozen cardboard kinds you throw in the oven. So she'd dressed in the denim jumper and drove into Durant to the Pizza Hut.

When she finished eating, she remembered she needed duct tape for sealing boxes, along with plastic garbage bags to wrap around the little cherry wood tables in the living room. So that brought her to the Wal-Mart. The tables would fit in her guest room, but she'd need to protect them if it happened to rain. Rain in August? Now wasn't that a dream? The only time it ever rained in August was the year she went to college, and that was a strange time, all around. She bought the duct tape and extra plastic bags, anyway. Could be that another weird time would bring rain in August.

And while I'm thinking about those tables, I think I'll get a drop cloth to cover that dresser in Aunt Bertha's bedroom. It'll match the antique bed that belonged to Mother. Most likely was bought at the same time as the end tables and the dresser. They all look the same. Bet Mother's dad got the bed at one time and Aunt Bertha kept the dresser and tables.

"Oh my!" a woman gasped as they practically ran

their two carts together at the end of the display. "Kitty?"

"Hello, Mrs. Fleming," she said softly. The woman had changed very little. Her hair might have a little more salt than pepper, but she still had a smooth complexion for a woman her age, and Kitty would have liked to hug her. It wasn't her fault her son was a rotten apple.

"What are you doing here?" The woman frowned angrily.

"I'm having an auction to sell Aunt Bertha's house and things. Next Friday."

"Your husband come with you?"

"No, I'm not married," Kitty said. She had scarcely even dated since Preston broke her heart, and in the space of ten minutes two people had asked her about her husband.

"Oh, didn't work out did it? Well, I'd say that was justice served right," Mrs. Fleming said bluntly. "Just don't go messing up my son's life again, Kitty Maguire. I wish he would've never come home on leave that summer. And we thought you were such a nice girl. Bertha was the salt of the earth, but I guess a leopard can't change its spots even with careful raising. Just stay away from Preston!" Her blue eyes snapped.

"What are you talking about?" Kitty asked.

"Oh, don't you play dumb with me, girl," the woman said, shaking her finger under Kitty's nose. "Just sell your stuff and go on back east where you belong." She turned the cart around and resolutely marched off.

Kitty stood in the middle of the store, pure bewilderment filling her soul as she tried to make sense of what Mrs. Fleming had said. It was as if she broke up with Preston, rather than the other way around. Suddenly the answers fell from the ceiling of the Wal-Mart and settled around her like a shroud.

That lousy, two-bit, two-timing rascal had brought his wife home and told everyone that Kitty had done *him* dirty. That's why those women in the Dairy Queen talked about her being ugly. She'd done him the tremendous favor of staying out of town for five years so he could build up a *poor Preston* image, wallowing in a soft, pampered existence because of his terrible misfortune with that devil of a woman, Kitty Maguire. And that's why Lisa could work up a hissy fit. Jody was still Preston's best friend, so they'd heard the story of how she'd been so terrible. Well, if her friend didn't trust her more than that, then she wouldn't bother her with the gory details of what really happened that summer. She'd just pack her truck, sell off the rest and go back to Oklahoma City where she belonged.

She smiled, just a hint of twinkle filtering back in her gray eyes. Maybe she'd just pay Preston a visit, though, and tell his little wife how the chips really fell that day in Trinidad. When he didn't even have the nerve to call back thirty minutes later and tell her himself that he'd fallen in love with another woman. Left a message with her aunt instead. When he never even cared enough to write her another letter to tell her that he'd had a major change of heart. At least Kitty had written him a pitiful letter in which she pleaded with him to reconsider, telling him that she loved him desperately. She'd put her whole heart into that letter, sitting up nearly all night writing it, leaving the tear stains where they fell so he'd realize how badly she hurt.

Kitty slammed a box of cereal into the cart. She'd laid her soul out. Bared it to the rock bottom. What did he think when he read those ten long, painful pages? Did he laugh and pitch them overboard?

She finished her shopping and was sliding into her pickup in the parking lot when she saw Preston. Her chest tightened up until she gasped for breath. Her palms were clammy and unshed tears stung her eyes. He was even more handsome than the picture branded in her memory. His broad shoulders and arms stretched his knit shirt to the fullest. His black hair was a little longer, brushed straight back, and she wanted to get out of her truck and run her fingers through it—maybe even drag his mouth down to hers in a searing kiss that would remind him of what they'd shared.

He was walking beside a tall blond woman and threw his arm around her shoulders familiarly. The woman shrugged it away and shook her head at him. It must be too hot for him to touch her.

"The day I shrugged off his touch would have been the day I had a visit with St. Peter at the Pearly Gates. But then I don't have to worry about that, do I? He made his choice and then saved face by laying all the blame on me." Kitty fired up the engine and backed out of the parking lot. When she was on the four lane highway going north, she stomped on the gas pedal and watched the gauge climb to eighty miles an hour before she let up.

Chapter Four

Kitty dressed carefully in an olive green, sleeveless linen dress and soft leather sandals with a strap the same color as the dress. She piled her chestnut brown hair up on top of her head in a bun, letting a few curls frame her face. If Preston and his wife were at Sunday morning mass then he could just deal with the fact she was there, too, and she hoped he was miserable the whole time. The sorry scoundrel anyway, acting like he did, then shifting the blame over to her.

The sad part was just the sight of him still made her insides melt into a pile of mush. She hadn't known that kind of feeling in so long she'd practically forgotten it. But she'd get rid of it faster than the old proverbial speeding bullet. Her job depended on cold hard facts and that was the way she intended to live her life. Not led around by the heartstrings like a teenage girl in love for the first time. She'd just simply have to face Preston and get over the past.

44

Had he really gone into architecture like they'd talked about? she wondered. She had enrolled with that as her major the first semester of college. By the second semester she didn't want anything to do with a career field that would bring Preston to mind every day. Then the government stepped in with an offer she latched onto. Her job as a profiler for the FBI became her life line, and she wouldn't give it up for anyone or anything. She'd worked hard for the agency and she loved the work she did. It made a difference in the big picture, as Timothy told her repeatedly.

She checked her reflection in the mirror above her old vanity one more time. Lipstick wasn't smeared. Hair wasn't falling down. At least she could go to church with a perfectly clear conscience. Preston probably hadn't even bothered to go to confession for his sins. Perhaps he didn't consider ruining a young girl's life a sin.

The red light caught her at the corner of University Boulevard. She tapped her fingers on the steering wheel as she listened to the middle of the Crook and Chase Country Countdown on the radio. They played an old Sara Evans tune, "Born to Fly." Was that why things happened the way they did that summer? Maybe Kitty Maguire was born to fly and all Preston Fleming would do was keep her on the ground.

"Nope." She shook her head. "I flew the highest with Preston. I would have had to put rocks in my pockets to keep my feet on the ground in those days. But I guess he wanted something closer to the ground, after all."

She drove past the southern boundary of the college.

Had Preston come home from the Navy and finished his education here. Would things have been different if she'd stayed in Bryan County and gone to school at Southeastern Oklahoma State?

Questions and questions. But no answers.

A few minutes later she nosed her truck into a parking spot in front of the St. Williams Catholic Church. A hundred fairies began to dance in her stomach when she opened the door of the church. What she really should do, she decided, was go back to Caddo, get out her note pad and profile her own self. She might find a few surprises if she ran a check on the emotional roller coaster she'd been on for the past three days. Thank goodness the auction was on Friday and she could get out of here once and for all.

She dipped her fingers in holy water and bent her knees in reverence before she entered the sanctuary. How could he even do those two holy things after telling such lies? She slid into the back pew just before services began. She listened to the priest and responded to the reading until she realized the whole Fleming family was sitting together in several pews right in front of her, and then she couldn't make herself think about spiritual things. Preston was so close that she could have thrown her prayer book and hit him. He was so hardheaded he probably wouldn't even feel it. Kate Fleming sat on the end of the pew with John, her husband, right beside her. Preston sat beside his father. His brother, Alan, was on the other side and his family lined up to next to him. Evidently the past five years had produced a couple more children for Alan and his wife, Christy. She saw another Fleming

son and his wife beside the children. The two pews
behind them held more Flemings. Kitty recognized
Preston's two sisters and a couple more brothers and
their families. Such a big, wonderful family and she'd
wanted so badly to be a part of it when she was in
love with Preston. *Was?* she asked herself, losing track
of what was being said. *Oh, all right, don't rub it in.
I admit I'm still so attracted to him that just looking
at his hair and shoulders gives me the hives. Where
is his big blond wife?*

The hair on the back of Preston's neck crawled.
Something or someone behind him wasn't quite right.
He wiggled in his seat, but hated to be rude and turn
around to see who was actually staring a hole in his
back. Alan elbowed him and mouthed for him to be
still, then grinned like when they were boys. Alan was
the oldest in the family, followed by four more brothers and two sisters. When everyone figured the Fleming family had contributed their last to the population
explosion, along came baby Preston and surprised
them all. So instead of one mother and father, he'd
actually had five brothers and two sisters who all
thought they had the right to boss him around.

He smiled at his older brother, but the antsy feeling
didn't go away. The only other time he felt like this
was when he was in the presence of Kitty Maguire.
Good grief! She had to be sitting behind him. Her blue
truck had been at the old Mason home place all weekend. He'd heard she was having an auction, but he
assumed it was over and she would have already gone
back east. New York? Pennsylvania? Just where back
east was it anyway? But, he'd be willing to bet dollars

to doughnuts she was somewhere behind him. She was at *his* church, listening to *his* priest deliver *his* Sunday morning mass. How dare she just waltz back into his part of Oklahoma, uninvited and unwanted. He wanted to kick something or someone.

Like it or not, just thinking about her being that close still made him short-winded. His mouth was so dry he had trouble uttering the responses to the reading. His heart stopped beating so long his chest ached, then it took off so fast he could hardly breathe. Was she sitting beside her husband? The man might not even know there had been someone in her life five years ago, but Preston vowed that he would before he got away from the church that morning. Preston fully well intended to walk right up to him, stick out his hand and introduce himself. It was high time that he got acquainted with the man who caused him to practically lose his mind. To see what the fellow looked like and to hear his voice. And Kitty could just slink back in a corner and like it or lump it. He'd teach her to invade his territory, just when he was finally getting over the dull ache in his heart. Or at least he thought he was getting over her. Evidently, he wouldn't ever know a moment's peace if just her presence in church could produce a lump the size of a baseball in his throat.

After mass, Kitty slipped out of the building before the hand shaking and visiting began. She opened the door to her truck and slid into the seat, and was just about to close the door when Preston appeared in front of the truck. How strange! Everyone wanted to tar and feather her or run her out of town on a bed rail. No

one wanted her to see poor Preston or upset his perfect
little world with his tall, blond wife, and yet from the
puzzled look on his face, he had something to say.
Maybe he was going to plead with her to leave town
and leave his spotless, shiny coat of armor intact.
Well, the begging days were past. She'd pleaded and
pleaded in pure humiliation when she mailed that letter, asking him to give her another chance.

She took a deep breath, opened the door, and
stepped outside. A hot breeze picked up a few wisps
of her hair and blew them across her face. Preston
almost reached out and brushed them back so he could
see her eyes more clearly. Mercy, but she was even
more beautiful than she'd been at eighteen. A gor-
geous woman stood before him in the place of the girl
he'd fallen in love with.

"Kitty?" he said flatly, hating his heart for pounding
so hard she could probably hear it.

"Preston?" she said back in the same voice, wishing
she could throw her arms around him and feel his lips
on hers. But he was married, and Kitty didn't play
those kind of games.

"Where's your husband?" he asked. "Is he not Catholic?"

"Where's your wife? She not Catholic?" she asked
right back.

"I asked first," he said.

"Well, my husband is probably in the same place
as your wife. Sitting on the front pew of the Baptist
or the Nazarene church. Or wherever she goes on Sunday morning," she shot back at him. "This is the new
world, Preston. People don't always marry inside their

faith. But then evidently you know that since your wife isn't here with you."

"Are you happy with the decision you made?" he asked.

"Are you?" She didn't give him an inch of room. Let him remember the way it really was when he made that phone call.

"I think we're talking in riddles." He cocked his head to one side.

"And the biggest one is yet to be solved, right?" she asked. "And that's the one of whether I'll tell what really happened that day you called from Trinidad and ruin your precious spotless reputation while I'm in Caddo, isn't it? I'm only here for a week, Preston. I'm getting rid of all of Aunt Bertha's things and then I'm going home. I won't say anything to upset your perfect little world or make you look bad before your friends. If you can live with yourself, then I can let you. Just don't come near me. I'll be gone by next Sunday, so I'll be sure to stay out of your way. So you stay away from me and I'll leave without telling the whole southern part of the state what a villain you really are."

"Kitty, what are you talking about?" he asked.

He looked like someone had just poleaxed him. His head was cocked to one side, his brows drawn down until those blue eyes were set deep. *That must go with the image of being the poor little mistreated boy next door*, Kitty thought.

"Let's start over. Are you still married?" he asked when she didn't answer.

"Still?" she said. "This isn't going to get us anywhere. Go home to your tall, blond wife, Preston." She wasn't telling him one thing.

"But . . ." He shook his head.

Kitty had a choice. She could keep arguing or she could cry. Preston wasn't going to have the satisfaction, even after five years, of seeing one tear smear her make-up. She turned away from him, got into her truck, and backed out, leaving him standing there with a frown.

The tears started when she reached the red light. She wiped them away with the back of her hand. Kitty Maguire didn't cry. In her job, she looked at the nastiest scenarios a human could create and coldly, methodically built a file on the person who perpetrated such violence. She was never, ever wrong. So why did she let Preston affect her like this? "Because he still owns part of my heart. I gave it to him and he kept it," she said.

She halfway expected to look in the rearview mirror and find him speeding after her. On second thought, though, why should he follow her? She'd told him she'd leave Caddo with his secret intact, so he didn't have a thing to worry about. When she got to the house, she looked down the road but he wasn't there. The wooden porch complained as she stomped across it and opened the door. So what if it squeaked? The people who bought the house could fix it. Right then, she could care less what was wrong with the old home place. She just wanted to be free of it and the pain in her heart.

She threw her purse in the rocking chair so hard that she broke her compact mirror. "Oh, great, just what I need. Seven years of bad luck!" she fussed as she picked up the pieces and pitched them in the trash can in the kitchen. *You know better than to let super-stition rule your life, Kitty Maguire. If every time a mirror got broke someone had bad luck there wouldn't be a single person who would cut mirrors. So stop thinking like that! Thinking about bad luck, though, why does everyone keep asking me where my husband is? Maybe it's the water. They all get crazy down here when they drink it. That makes as much sense as su-perstition over a crazy mirror, I suppose,* she thought.

She left her dress in a heap on the floor at the foot of the bed, and jerked a faded T-shirt over her head. She pulled on a pair of cut offs and padded into her aunt's room to go through the dresser. She'd planned on eating at a restaurant in Durant, but she didn't want to look at another Fleming and there was always the possibility they were going out to eat after mass. It would be just her luck to walk into the same restaurant where they'd chosen to have lunch. She made herself a ham and cheese sandwich and took it to Aunt Ber-tha's bedroom. She nibbled on the corner of the sand-wich, made herself chew and swallow, then laid it aside. Her nervous stomach wasn't having another bite until it settled down.

She pulled out the first drawer . . . underwear, cot-ton, size nine, all white. Now what should she do with all that? She couldn't put her aunt's underpants in an auction, and they were too good to toss in the trash. She shut it and pulled out the next drawer . . . night-gowns, some flannel, some batiste, all floral. Wouldn't those elderly ladies have a hay day on the gossip line if they came to the auction and found that the ugly, insensitive Kitty Maguire had put her great aunt's lingerie up for sale?

"How much would you give me for this flannel nightgown?" She picked up one with pink rosebuds all over it. She giggled, out of nervousness more than humor. "Will it bring as much as the antimassacars which are already starched and ready for use?"

She shut that drawer, too. There wasn't much sentiment about what was in the dresser drawers, at least. There might be something before she got finished to bring on a tear or two, but nothing in the dresser. She opened the third drawer. Sweaters . . . cardigans with all the buttons still intact. A pink one, two blue ones and a white lacy one Bertha wore to church.

She picked them up and noticed a manila envelope underneath. The edges of several letters were peeping out, and it was addressed to Aunt Bertha. The return address was from Katherine Mason Maguire and dated twenty years earlier. "Good grief," Kitty exclaimed. "She's kept letters Mother wrote all the way back when I was a little girl." Kitty didn't bother to look inside at the letters. She just slipped the whole folder back in the drawer.

I'm taking this dresser home with me anyway, so there's no need to empty it before I go, she thought. *Besides, I can donate all the sweaters and nightgowns*, she decided.

Preston turned around in the parking lot to see half his family staring at him from the front of the church. Nothing could have ever prepared him for the way he'd felt when he looked at Kitty again. Not one thing she said made a bit of sense, yet he could have stood there and listened to her for hours. Just to hear her voice, even when filled with anger, made his heart soar.

"Well, what did Kitty Maguire have to say to you?" his mother asked when he rejoined his family.

"Who knows?" He faked a grin. "Something about not telling what a rascal I was while she was in town. I'm not sure what she was talking about."

"Well, I saw her in Wal-Mart yesterday," his mother said. "I told her to stay away from you, Preston. We don't need her kind around us. Now let's go home and eat lunch."

"I can take care of myself." Preston cocked his head to one side. "What else did you say to her?"

"I just asked her if her husband came with her." Kate didn't back down an inch from her son.

"And?"

"She said she wasn't married, so I guess it didn't work out. Surprise. Surprise. The way she treated you, I hope she got dumped. I hope he saw right through her and broke her heart just like she did yours."

"So she's not married now? Did she say where she lives or what she does for a living?"

"According to what she said, she's not married. But that doesn't mean she's up for grabs to you, son," Kate said. "We're a family. We took care of you when you came home all broken-hearted. You know the saying, 'Burn me once, shame on you. Burn me twice, shame on me.' Well, we won't gather 'round and take care of you again if you let that awful woman tear you up again. And honey, I don't care if she lives in a million dollar mansion or a two room shack without a bathroom. She's pure trouble and you stay away from her."

"And that's a fact," his brother Alan chipped in. "You know what she is. Stay away from her."

"Whew." Preston smiled. "Advice must be a nickel a bushel this morning and y'all bought a hundred dollars worth. Frankly, I'm not overly worried about my love life right now. I'm worried about my stomach, so could we go home and eat?"

Preston was glad the subject of Kitty Maguire didn't come up again at the table. He told them all he needed a nap and was going home when the meal was finished. But instead, he drove slowly past the old Mason house. Her blue truck was in the driveway. Why had she kept the truck all those years if she'd remarried? Surely she didn't want a reminder of his blue eyes when she was married to another man.

When he got home, he changed from his three-piece, western-cut suit into a pair of cut offs and a baggy T-shirt. Pouring himself a glass of cold sweet tea, he let the memories of that summer begin to flood around his heart. He carried the tea to the deck and stretched his long, muscular frame out in his favorite chaise lounge, but he didn't go to sleep. Instead, he replayed every memory of Kitty Maguire he could conjure up from those thirty days when he came home on leave from the Navy.

In spite of his mother's warnings, by nightfall he had decided that he was going to that auction on Friday. He might even buy the old Mason home place just to show Kitty Maguire that he could.

Chapter Five

The truck was piled high and covered with a bright yellow plastic tarp. The back yard looked like a dumping ground with stuff in boxes, set on tables and scattered everywhere. The auctioneer would arrive any moment and Kitty was absolutely relieved to be finally selling the whole thing. She'd gone through drawers and cabinets until she was bone-tired and weary. By noon she hoped to be on the way to Oklahoma City to her apartment, Caddo and all its memories safely locked away.

She pulled on a pair of jeans and a T-shirt, ate a powdered sugar doughnut from a box and drank a can of orange juice for breakfast, and sat down on the back porch to wait. The two ladies from the Dairy Queen arrived first. They nodded toward Kitty without actually speaking. She watched them go from item to item. No doubt, they were looking for the little cherry wood end tables. Well, they'd just have to make do with the antimassacars.

"Hello, Kitty."

She'd been so engrossed in watching the two ladies prowl through the boxes that she hadn't even heard Preston's footsteps. His voice made the hair on her arms tingle. The warm breath that caressed the tender flesh right under her ear practically made her lose her vow to never mess with a married man.

"Preston?" she said coolly.

"Got good news and bad news." He grinned down at her. Blue jeans and a T-shirt and not five pounds heavier than she'd been when she was eighteen. He longed to take her in his arms and just hold her for two minutes to listen to her heart beat in unison with his.

"Oh?" She raised an eyebrow. Caddo did not have good news to offer Kitty Maguire, and the entirety of the bad news was that Preston was on her property.

"Bad news is that your auctioneer, Richard Sampson, and his wife got a phone call last night. Their daughter, Rochelle, has decided to have her baby a month early. So they're at an Oklahoma City hospital this morning. He called me at midnight. Good news is that I do fill-in auctioneer work for Rich and he asked me to hold this auction so you aren't left with no one to take care of it. Only problem is his wife usually does the book work. I've got the numbers." He opened a briefcase and took out a clipboard and a sheaf of papers. "If you'll be my bookkeeper we can go on with this sale."

"I'd rather eat toad frogs," she snapped.

"Then I'll go home and you can haul all this stuff right back in the house and wait until Rich can get down here," he said gruffly. Dang it all! The woman had broken his heart and here she was five years later acting like she was the Queen of blasted Sheba. Like he wasn't even good enough to hold an auction for her.

"No," she said with a shake of the head. She was a grown woman and she worked with people who riled her all the time. Even though she loved Jasper, he made her so angry on a daily basis that she prayed homicide would be declared legal just so she could shoot him. Come to think of it, maybe if it was ever declared legal, she'd shoot Preston first and then Jasper if he was on her bad list that day. Preston would stay at the top of her list . . . forever and ever. "I'll do it. I want this sale over and finished today. Where is your wife?"

"Preston, what are you doing here? Tammy going to help you?" one of the DQ ladies asked incredulously.

"No, Tammy's not going to help me. But I'm running the auction today, with Kitty's help. You ladies going to bid? You need to pick up your numbers," he said. "Folks?" He stood on the porch and yelled to get everyone's attention in the back yard. "The sale will begin in fifteen minutes. Kitty has the numbers and registration right here. Step right up here and get a number or you won't be able to bid. Nine o'clock sharp, we're going to take off with that washer and dryer right over there." He pointed.

So Tammy was his wife's name. The tall blonde who'd shrugged off his arm in the Wal-Mart parking lot. She wasn't Catholic or else she was home sick last Sunday and she didn't help him with auctions. Kitty methodically gave out numbers and registered bidders as she quickly built a profile of Preston's wife. Uncaring. Not warm. Trusting to let him come to Kitty Maguire's place to serve as auctioneer. Beautiful.

"Hey, Preston, these things in working order?" a man called from the area where the washer and dryer were sitting.

"Were last time Miss Bertha used them, I'd say," he said, strolling across the yard. "You know she took care of everything real well. You going to bid on this set, Joe?"

"Might. Wife says hers is ready to bite the dust and don't want her to get riled up. You know what they say, 'If Momma ain't happy, ain't nobody happy,' so I wouldn't want her to get het up cause she can't get the Monday washin' done up." He laughed and a round woman with slightly purple hair poked him in the ribs.

"How come you're doing this auction? I figured you'd run a country mile to keep away from here today," the woman asked in hushed tones.

"Just doin' Rich a favor," he said. "What went on five years ago is old history."

And that's where it's going to stay, Kitty thought when she walked up beside him. "Hello, Mr. Johnson. I just used the washer and dryer last night so it's in working order. I think everyone has numbers now,

Preston," she said in a business-like tone. "Are we ready?"

"Ten, nine, eight . . ." He looked at his watch dramatically and began the countdown.

"Seven, six, five . . ." He grinned.

Kitty's head reeled just inhaling his familiar aftershave. If she made it though the day she was going to give herself a medal for behavior above and beyond the call of duty. She might even tell Jasper, when she got back to the field office, that she deserved another vacation day for keeping her cool in a very difficult situation.

"Four, three, two." He dragged out the last number, teasing the crowd and loving every minute that he could stand beside Kitty Maguire. He'd give half his ranch to know exactly what happened between her and the Yankee so that the marriage didn't work. Or, perhaps it never happened. Now wouldn't that be poetic justice if she'd thrown Preston over for someone else, and that man didn't want her after all.

"One. The bidding will begin." He dropped his arm.

Kitty followed it down to his side, and while he rambled on and on so fast she couldn't begin to understand, she eyed him. From the tips of his well-polished black eel cowboy boots, up the starched, tight-fitting jeans, to the big silver belt buckle with a bronc rider on it. So he was still doing the rodeos, was he? Did Tammy ride also? Maybe a little barrel racing, or perhaps with her size and the fact that she was an ex-military person, she might even do ladies' bull riding. Did his wife always push him away or would she meet him at the door of their home that evening, grab the bottom snap of that fancy, western-cut white shirt, and undo all the snaps with one flick of the wrist? Jealously filled Kitty, making her set her mouth and draw her eyebrows down until they were almost a solid line across her gray eyes.

"Sold! To number fifteen. Joe, you just made Momma a happy woman," Preston teased. "Now, we'll sell this box of . . . stuff." He laughed. "Kitty, you want to tell the folks what you got in this box right here? Looks like those lacy things Miss Bertha put on her chair backs."

"Antimassacars and doilies. Freshly starched and ready for use," she said, looking out over the crowd. The two DQ ladies perked right up and made their way to the front line.

"What do we start at? Can I hear five dollars for the whole box? I got a five right there. Now how about six?" He started the fast talk again.

The words to the song she'd heard on the way to church the previous Sunday came to her mind. Sara Evans singing about being born to fly. What would her life have been like if she'd continued to fly with Preston? Would they have children by now? Would she have been an architect after all, instead of a government agent?

"Sold to number six!" he finally shouted. "Mrs. Quaid, you just barely got them. I thought Darlene was going to outbid you. You ladies ought to share the cost and split the box." He continued to tease them and Kitty almost choked. Darlene and Mrs. Quaid. They really were the DQ ladies.

"Now let's go right on down the line. This coffee

table looks like an antique to me. Solid oak. They don't build them like this anymore, do they? Can I hear twenty-five dollars to start? No, well then let's start at fifteen and climb from there. I got a fifteen, now how about a twenty?" He was off again.

It wasn't so difficult. She would have been crazy to call the auction off just because he was the one to do the selling. All those years when she'd awakened in the still of the night, in a cold sweat following a dream about him, and here she stood so close she could smell the peppermint gum he chewed all the time. And it wasn't difficult at all. Yes, there was a twinge in her heart; a pulling of the strings tight enough to make a little pain. But then he was standing so close she could smell his aftershave and watch a little stream of sweat roll down his square face and drip from his strong jawbone onto his shirt. But it wasn't something she couldn't endure. He would do his job; she would do hers. She'd pay him and he could go home to his wife, Tammy, who might not even want to tear off his shirt when he got home that evening because it smelled of a day's sweat created by honest work.

I would, she thought. *I wouldn't care if he had worked all day. I'd unsnap that shirt and run my fingers through all that soft black hair on his chest and be as happy as a kid in a candy store. But he made his choice, so he can just live with his cold-hearted woman who doesn't even want his arm around her shoulders on a hot day.*

At exactly noon, Preston checked his watch and turned to Kitty. "Is that the whole she-bang?" he asked. "Got any more stuff in the house or change your mind about what's under the tarp in that blue truck?"

"No, that's it. I'll set up shop on the porch and collect the money and they can haul their goods away." She was proud of herself for keeping a non-committal tone in her voice.

"The lady says that's the sale, folks. Thanks for coming out today and making the sale go fast. Load up your purchases and pay Kitty on the back porch." He laid his cordless microphone down and picked up a Dr. Pepper from a mini-cooler at his feet.

"Care for one?" he asked Kitty.

"No, thank you." She would have loved a cold drink but she didn't want to take even the slightest chance of his hand brushing against hers.

"Hot work," he mumbled.

"Hey, Preston, you ain't selling the house on the auction block?" Joe asked.

"You interested in buying it?" Preston grinned, deepening the cleft in his chin.

"Nope, just wondering," Joe said. "Heard Mrs. Smith's place and this one were both for sale. Just wondered if you was going to try to auction them to-day."

"They've already sold. Bought yesterday from the real estate agency," Preston told him.

Kitty jerked her head around. The agent hadn't pho-ned her or come by yesterday to show the house to anyone. Besides, how in the devil did Preston know so much about the deal? *The Caddo gossip line*, she remembered. Everyone knew everything. At least the folks who'd lived there since the sixth day of creation.

Newcomers had a hard time breaking into the system, but the old timers knew everything within five minutes after it happened.

"Who'd they sell to? Agency buy them for rent houses?" Joe's wife asked.

"I bought them both," Preston answered, but he was careful to keep his eyes on Kitty. He wouldn't miss her reaction to that news for all the dirt in Texas.

"What are you going to do with two old frame houses?" Joe asked as a silence filled the back yard. "Going to go into the rentin' business?"

Kitty didn't disappoint him. If looks could kill he would have fallen down and been ready for the undertaker to carry his carcass away to the funeral home. She shot him a look that let him know he'd done exactly what he intended. To get under her skin and make her as mad as he'd been the whole week.

"Nope, going to run an ad in the paper next week. Going to sell them both cheap to someone to move them off this property. I'm donating the land to the school for a new softball field," he said quietly.

Kitty seethed. How dare he buy the house? *Oh, hush*, she chided herself. *I wouldn't care if Santa Claus bought the place for a new doll factory. So why do I care if Preston Fleming buys it for a softball field?*

"Needed a tax write off did you?" Another man chuckled.

"You bet I did." Preston nodded.

"Miss Maguire?" The real estate agent was the last one in line when she looked up. "Sorry I wasn't here for the auction. I just came to tell you that I sold the house yesterday. Meant to run by and tell you, but my daughter had a softball game and time got away from me. If you'll come by the office on your way out of town, you can sign all the papers and I'll write you a check."

"Thank you," she said. "I'll be another hour or so here waiting for the folks to get finished and then I'll be on my way. One o'clock?"

"That will be great," he said. "Oh, Fleming Architectural Firm bought the place if you're interested to know. Bought it and the one next door. Going to turn this whole corner into a softball field for the school."

"That's nice." She stood up and handed Preston the clipboard. "Thank you for selling it. Thank you, Preston, for buying it. Now I won't have to ever make another trip back to this forsaken place."

Miss Maguire, the man had called her. So she either hadn't ever married the fellow out east or else she took her maiden name back when she divorced him or he threw her out, whatever the case might be. She could thank him until the moon dripped green cheese and the words wouldn't mean a blessed thing. He knew she was really angry. Her gray eyes were as cold as a winter sky after a hard snow.

"You are quite welcome, Miss Maguire." He drew the last two words out. "Shall we grab a hamburger to celebrate the job being finished?"

"No thank you. I've got a few more things to do in the house and then I'm leaving. Good-bye, Preston," she said curtly as she slammed the back door behind her.

"Whew!" Rick, the real estate agent wiped his brow.

"Pretty cold woman. You make her mad before the auction or did you sell things too cheap?"

"Made her mad. But then she made me mad about five years ago. Funny world we live in, Rick. Had dinner yet?"

"Yes, the wife and I already had lunch. Want to meet me in the office at one and sign the final draft on this land? Might as well get it all done before she leaves. I don't think she plans to leave one thing in Caddo that she might have to come back for. Man, I don't know that I've ever seen anyone hate this area so much. But then I guess them big city folks who work for the government are too classy for the likes of us," Rick said quietly.

"Government? Is that what she does? Design houses for the government?" Preston asked as they walked around to the front of the house together.

"Nope, she don't design nothing, Preston. She works for one of those government agencies. CIA or FBI or something like that. I asked her what she did and she just said it was very secret and very governmental. Only time she made a joke the whole time I been dealing with her. Said, 'I could tell you what I do but then I'd have to kill you.' You know, like in the movies."

"I see," Preston said. She hadn't followed in her mother's footsteps after all. Or continued with the dream the two of them had shared when they were engaged, either. They were going to build the biggest, best architectural firm in the whole state of Oklahoma. Either her father or the eastern man must have had some kind of political pull to get her a government job. He wondered if she worked in Washington, DC and just what she did do?

Kitty sat down in the middle of the floor in her old bedroom. She could see the driveway from her window. She'd leave when Preston was gone. She had loaded everything into her truck the night before. All but the big brown bear. She had slept with it the last night in her room. Then that morning she had carefully taken down her bed and put it outside in the back yard to be auctioned off.

There wasn't any way she was leaving the bear in the house for Preston to see when he brought prospective buyers inside. She couldn't leave it and she couldn't carry it out in front of him. Either way he would know that she hadn't destroyed the silly thing all those years ago. Finally, she saw him and Rick walk across the front yard and stand beside their pickup trucks for a while. They were deep in conversation and Preston kept looking toward the house. As if he could see past the walls and into the room. As if he could see the interior of her heart and know the effect just his presence had had on her all day.

Wouldn't Jasper laugh his bald head off if he could see his prize agent sitting on the floor of an old house in a little southern Oklahoma town, hugged up next to a big brown teddy bear and waiting for an old love to go home so she could leave. It did make a pretty funny picture if she was honest with herself. Suddenly she was ready to go home to Oklahoma City. Ready for an assignment. She'd beg Jasper to send her away for a couple of weeks. California. New York. DC, it didn't matter. Just so long as she had twenty-eight hours of work to do in every twenty-four hour span and didn't have time to think about Preston Fleming again.

Chapter Six

Kitty grabbed the door handle to the real estate agency about the same time Preston opened it from the inside. She jumped back and he stepped outside before he realized she was even there. His arm brushed hers and the sparks flying between them rivaled the Independence Day fireworks display. A vision of his mouth stringing kisses up the tender skin on her wrist all the way to her elbow, then taking her in his arms and sliding his tongue across her lower lip, materialized. She shivered in spite of the hundred-degree heat the thermometer proclaimed.

"Pardon me?" He took a deep breath. So much for never feeling that way again. She still had the power to make him turn into a bumbling fool just by the simple touch of her bare arm against his.

"I didn't realize you were on your way out," she said. "Good-bye again."

"Kitty, could we talk?" he asked.

"I don't think that's a good idea." She went inside the agency without looking back. Mercy, but she hoped he didn't take a peek inside her truck and see the bear propped up in the passenger seat.

In fifteen minutes she'd signed every place Rick pointed to and was sitting in her truck. The bear couldn't tell her whether it had had a visitor or not. "Well, it's over," she said. "All finished, kaput. I'm going home, Bear. If you're a good boy you can stay with me for awhile. Maybe I'll find some little kid who needs a good bear to keep him safe. To cuddle up with at night. Someone to tell his troubles to. You just might come in handy. One last thing, though, you'll have to sit in the truck alone for a spell before we go. I'm having a big greasy hamburger before I leave. One for the road, so to speak."

There was a parking spot right in front of the Dairy Queen. The lunch crowd had already been there and gone back to work. No one turned to look at her when she pushed the door open. No one except Preston Fleming, who was sitting in a back booth eating a bacon cheeseburger. He laid his food down and folded his arms across his chest. Just when he thought he was over her forever and for good, there she was every time he turned around.

Tammy had called him the night before to ask him just what was wrong. He hadn't been himself lately. He hadn't phoned all week. Did they still have a date for Friday? He'd told her he had an auction to call and didn't know when it would be finished, so they'd better cancel the movies and dinner. What he should have said was that he didn't care if he ever saw her again.

That whether he ever had one of her quick kisses again didn't matter any more.

Kitty waited at the counter until they brought her food. Then she turned to find Preston staring right at her. He didn't even glance away, just continued to rudely look his fill. She fought down the urge to tell the girl behind the counter to make her order to go after all, but she wasn't going to let him run her out of Caddo before she ate her lunch. She chose a booth beside the front door and sat down with her back to him. He could look all he wanted . . . at her hair and shoulders. She picked up the burger and bit into it, but it tasted like a rice cake. The chocolate malt had even less flavor. But she was going to eat every last french fry and drink the malt to the bottom.

She made herself swallow the second bite. Her scalp prickled. She wasn't going to feel that way again. Not ever. Yet, here she was with a case of hives caused by a married man staring at her. She needed to get back to her own world where she could forget Preston.

"Good-bye, Kitty. Sure we can't find time to talk?" He stood so close behind her she could feel his warm breath on her neck. She shivered and goosebumps raised up on her arms.

"I don't think it would accomplish a single thing. Good-bye again, Preston," she said coldly, without looking at him—at least not until he was out the door and getting into his truck.

He tipped his hat to her and grinned when he caught her watching him. A slow heat crawled up the back of her neck and brought two spots of high color to her cheeks. She waited until he was gone, dumped the rest of her food into the trash and drove north out of Caddo. It was past time to forget all about Preston Fleming.

"Right!" she moaned and thought about him the whole three hours to her apartment. She backed the truck up to the edge of the sidewalk and was glad to see one of her single neighbors and a couple of his young college friends stop their touch football game and jog over.

"Here, we'll take this stuff in for you. What'd you do? Find an auction somewhere? Great Scott, Miss Kitty, you got a stash of gold in this thing?" He laughed as he and his buddies carried Aunt Bertha's dresser up the stairs to her apartment.

"You might say that. Of course it's not loaded with gold. It's loaded with rocks. I just wanted to see how strong you boys are," she teased right back. "Put it in my guest bedroom. Right here." She hurried ahead of them to open the door and show them where to place it.

A bottom drawer slid open when they tilted it to get it through the door. The packet of letters flew out onto the floor. She shoved them back inside the drawer without even looking at them. Tomorrow she would toss them in the trash and donate the rest of the things. Right then she had to tell the guys where to put the rest of her inheritance while they were still willing to help unload the truck.

When the job was done, she collapsed in the middle of the living room floor. She kicked off her shoes and wiggled her toes in the thick carpet. Boxes were everywhere but she didn't care. She was home. She folded her hands behind her head and shut her eyes. An hour's nap. That's what she needed. But the vision her mind conjured up wasn't conducive to sleeping. There was Preston in his tight-fitting jeans and silver belt buckle with a cordless microphone in his hand, calling the auction. Or there he was in his three-piece suit after church services.

"Well, rats!" She snapped her eyelids open to make the picture go away. "Jasper better have something really good for me so I can get that married man off my mind."

When she walked through the doors at 8:30 on Monday morning, Jasper grinned like the cat who'd found the door to the canary cage wide open. Kitty could almost see the yellow feathers hanging out of his mouth.

"Maguire, thank goodness you're back. There's a situation in Dallas, honey. David, get on the phone. I want a ten o'clock flight for Kitty. Go home and pack enough for a week or two. David will pick you up in time to catch the plane."

"Brief me." She followed him to the office. "Weapon?"

"Not on the plane. Not even for you. Security is tighter these days, and rightly so." He shook his head. "They'll supply it for you in Dallas. I told them you liked a .38 special. They laughed. Said they'd have a Glock ready. I think I made them understand you don't work with one of their fancy weapons. I don't really think you'll need one anyway. They just need your insight on a profile. I'm not briefing you on anything.

They'll show you the pictures and what they've got so far. Too bad you couldn't take in the crime scene before it was contaminated. But they've got hundreds of pictures. You can put them in the overhead projector and work your way around the room and house that way. Also got samples of everything from dirt on the floor to dust bunnies from under the bed. I want you to approach it with all you've got."

"Yes, sir." She grinned. This was exactly what the doctor ordered. Good hard work. Big city. No one she knew. That meant she could work sixteen to twenty hours a day without interruption. "I'm glad to have something to plow right into."

"And I'm glad to have you behind the plow." Jasper rubbed his bald head and adjusted his wire-rimmed glasses. His blue eyes, set in a bed of wrinkles, twinkled. "I've got a dozen agents and as many profilers. But you take a look at a case and you can tell me what the perp had for breakfast. How he eats his omelets and whether or not he shared a bedroom with his brother when he was six years old. That's what they need down there. So get on out of here. Call me if you need anything."

"Thanks, Jasper," she said.

"I forgot to ask about the sale, I was so excited to see you a day early. Did it go all right down there?"

"Went fine. It's sold, signed, and over, and I'm ready to go to work."

"Welcome home," he said. "Check in on Friday and let me know if you need anything."

"Maybe some magic," she said with a grin.

"You don't need anything that silly," Jasper said.

"You've got a mind like a bear trap. You sure don't need any voodoo."

She grinned back at him as she picked up her purse and went back to the apartment to pack a bag. She dragged out her trusty old black suitcase and tossed in what she needed for a couple of weeks. Couple of basic black pantsuits, jeans and T-shirts, a plain sweat-suit for the hotel exercise room. That's one thing she always insisted on, a place to get rid of the stress after long, hard hours. A bathing suit in case she had time for a swim before breakfast. She shook her head when she carried the suitcase to the living room. Boxes and garbage bags were still scattered everywhere, the bear was on the easy chair, and she shuddered to think about the guest room.

"That's what I get for lazing around last night. I'll clean it all up when I get home. I'll be ready for it then." She sighed as she locked the door to her apart-ment.

Preston didn't know how long he'd been sitting in the dark on his deck. He'd said the words "good-bye," but he didn't feel them. He didn't want it to be final. Not anymore. Not since he'd seen her and felt the sparks that lit up the whole town when he touched her. But it really was final, whether he wanted to admit it or not. She'd turned up out of the clear blue sky and disappeared the same way. She would be back east by now, he figured. It had been three days. He'd spent the weekend doing nothing but sitting on the deck with a glass of sweet tea and wishing he could see her again.

He was at the firm at six o'clock on Monday morning. Good, hard, mind-boggling work was what he needed. He would stay with it until he couldn't hold his eyes open another minute, then go home at midnight. Yes, sir, Preston had it all under control. At six that evening he closed the doors. His project wasn't finished, but he couldn't make any progress. Even the angle of a pencil line reminded him of Kitty. So he went home, poured another glass of tea and went to his favorite chaise lounge. He had been sitting on the deck so long that the ice in his tea had long since melted when he heard the crunch of gravel under the wheels of a vehicle out front.

"Preston? Are you out back, honey?" Tammy called from the front door.

"On the deck." He raised his voice slightly. Her high-heeled shoes beat out a rat-a-tat noise on the hard wood as she crossed the floor. He surely did not want to see Tammy that night. He wasn't sure he ever wanted to see another woman again.

"Hi," She pulled up a chaise lounge and stretched her long, lanky frame out beside him. "I thought I'd better come see if you were alive."

"Barely," he said.

"Sick?"

"Nope, just discontent," he said.

"Got anything to do with that Maguire woman who had the auction? Your sister told me you were pretty hung up on her at one time and she threw you over for some fellow back east with a lot of money," Tammy said.

"Probably," he nodded.

"Well, I've come to take care of poor old Preston." She giggled. "We've been seeing each other for a few months and I think it's time we got engaged. We can plan a Christmas wedding. You know, one of those things where there's real live trees at the front of the church and poinsettias everywhere. You don't have any objections to getting married at my church, do you? I just wouldn't feel right in the Catholic church. I've been Methodist all my life."

"No!" He bolted straight up.

"Good." She patted his hand. She wouldn't tell him that she'd already seen a real estate agent about an old, two-story brick home on Main Street in Durant, or that she'd met with an interior decorator that afternoon. That could all come in due time. After a few weeks of engagement, and nearer the wedding. "Then it's all settled. We'll go buy me a big engagement ring tomorrow."

"No!" he said again when he found his voice. He wasn't going to settle for anything less than the jolt of electricity that flowed through him when he touched Kitty. Not one inkling less. He might be a cantankerous old bachelor, but he wasn't going to marry Tammy and regret the decision the rest of his life. No, he was going to find Kitty Maguire and they were going to have a long talk.

"No engagement ring?" She cocked her head to one side.

"No, I'm not going to marry you," he said bluntly. "I'm a hermit and I love this ranch and I'm not interested in getting married. Not now. Besides, Tammy, I don't love you, and marriage is a hard job even when it's built around love. It's just a statistic waiting for the divorce courts when it's not."

"Well, Preston, I thought we were an item around here. I thought we were just waiting for the right time," she jumped up so quick she knocked over the end table where his tea was sitting. It spilled in his lap and he was on his feet as fast as he could.

"I never asked you to marry me, nor did I lead you on to expect that we would marry, Tammy. You're a city person and could never be happy on my ranch. I'm a country boy at heart, and would never be content but right here. We don't fit together, Tammy," he said. "I thought we were just two adults enjoying a little company."

"You can just live out here with the coyotes and dogs then, Preston Fleming. I came out here to save you from disgrace. Everyone is already talking about how that Maguire woman can wrap you around her finger even after the way she treated you. Don't say I didn't try to help you. We could be good together. I suppose I could live out here on this forsaken place if that's what you really want." She'd make him change his mind . . . no matter what it took.

"No thank you, Tammy. I don't mean to be rude, but I'm not . . ."

"Then I'm leaving," she said. "Don't come crying to me when she breaks your heart again. I was a fool to think I could help you anyway."

"I'm sorry," he apologized and wondered just what he had done wrong.

"You sure are." She stormed out of the house, slamming the front door as she left and slinging gravel all over the porch as she spun out of the driveway in her little sports car.

Preston calmly picked up the phone directory and found the number he'd needed. Rick, the real estate agent, answered on the third ring. "Hello," he said groggily.

"Sorry, Rick. Did I wake you?"

"Just barely. I'd fallen asleep during the game on television. What you needin' Preston? Got someone interested in buying those two houses already?"

"No, I need to know Kitty Maguire's phone number or address," he said. "I know she probably gave them to you since you were going to list her house."

"Got them down at the agency. Don't have them here. Is it a breach of confidence or something if I give them to you? That woman looked mean enough to do some damage to a person who double-crossed her." He chuckled.

"I'll come by tomorrow morning, first thing," Preston said. "If she sues you I'll pay the bill. You remember what state she's living in? Pennsylvania or DC or . . ."

"Oh, no," Rick said. "She lives in Oklahoma City. Works for the FBI field office there. Gave me her work number and her apartment number. Apartment is unlisted so I'd best keep it from you. Guess the work number is public domain. You could probably get it yourself by calling information."

"Oklahoma City? Are you sure?" Preston asked incredulously.

"Sure, I'm sure. She said she's been there ever since she graduated from college. Did all kinds of night courses and everything to finish up early and then got a master's degree in psychology or criminology or something like that. Been working on her doctorate, she said, in her spare time. Government trained her the whole time. Does some kind of special work but didn't go into it. I barely got that much out of her. Told her she was too young to work for that kind of place."

"But how'd she get out here from the east coast?" Preston wondered aloud.

"East coast. Don't know about that. She started school in Tulsa and finished at Oklahoma University," Rick said.

"Tulsa?" Preston frowned into the phone.

"Yep, see you tomorrow if you haven't gotten what you want from information," he said.

"Thanks, Rick." Preston hung up and went back out to the deck to try to make sense of what he'd just learned.

The next morning he marched into his office without even saying hello to his brothers who were having coffee around the conference table. He went back into his private office, dialed a couple of numbers, and waited.

"Federal Bureau of Investigation," a man said on the other end.

"Kitty Maguire, please," he said tersely.

"Kitty is out of the office for a few days. Could I take a message?"

"I need to get in touch with her. Could you give me a number where she might be reached?"

"May I ask who's calling?"

"This is Preston Fleming, an old friend of Kitty's and I . . ."

"I'm sorry. Kitty is out of state for awhile. I can give her a message when she returns, sir, but you cannot contact her right now," the man said.

"Then when she comes home, please tell her that Preston called. I would appreciate it if she would call me back at any of these numbers. This one is my home. This is my business and this is my cell phone. I can be reached anywhere, anytime, night or day," he said.

"I'll give her the message," the man said.

Preston stormed out of the office and kicked a small metal trash can across the room. The noise it made when it hit the far wall and clattered across the tile floor did nothing to soothe his anger. "Gone out of state," he mumbled to his brothers.

"Is Kitty Maguire responsible for this outrage?" Alan asked.

"Yes, she is," he snorted. "FBI, unlisted home phone number, can't get her address. Gone for two weeks to lord only knows where and I'm miserable."

"What do you intend to do?" Alan asked. "Kill a trash can or two a day?"

"Wait," Preston moaned. "I intend to wait. But I'm going to have it out with that girl. I don't care if it's in two weeks or two months. She's going to listen to what I've got to say."

"What about what Momma has to say?" Alan asked.

"Momma is going to have to let me get this straightened out however I can," he said. "Something isn't right. She never did go back east. She went to college in Tulsa and at OU. All this time she's been close enough I could have driven to see her and I didn't know it. She still goes by Kitty Maguire so she probably never did even marry the fellow Aunt Bertha told me about. It's driving me crazy."

Alan shook his head. "She drove you crazy before. You've just been getting back to normal this past year and now she comes to town for a week and you're right back to square one. Brother, you better get that woman out of your head so you can go on living. I'm not telling Momma a thing. You do what you got to do. It don't matter to me. I just want to see you happy again."

"That's exactly what I want." Preston sighed. "You can't know how much I want to be happy again. But I'm not sure I'll ever feel that way again. Not in this lifetime. Kitty owns half my heart and the other half don't know how to live without her."

Chapter Seven

Jasper looked up from his desk to find Kitty leaning on the door jamb. She looked like she'd been the only chicken at a two-week coyote party. Her eyes had dark circles under them. Her expression said she was sleeping on her feet right then.

"Well, look what the dogs have dragged up." He smiled.

"And the cats wouldn't have," she finished the cliché for him. "I told you to get me a place cleared off for a fit but I'm too tired to pitch a hissy. I want Monday off," she said bluntly.

"You don't even have to throw a tantrum, darlin'." He grinned. "It was a rough case, but it's in the bag. Perp is behind bars. Maguire's calculations did it again. You got Monday. Take the rest of this afternoon, too. Go home. Sleep all weekend and Monday as well. I'll see you on Tuesday."

"Jasper, I almost didn't figure it out. The pictures

and the lab reports didn't give me enough, so I went out to the crime scene to snoop around on my own. I wanted to see if there was anything the lab or the pictures might have missed. The killer decided to come back at the same time. He had a ten-inch fillet knife. I had to shoot him in the leg. It was scary as the devil, Jasper. Those ten minutes lasted twenty years." She melted into an easy chair.

"Want to talk about it? Need to go visit the counselor?" Jasper looked worried.

"No to both. I'd look at the pictures, but all I could see was Preston Fleming. I figured if I could sit in the middle of the scene, I could see things without him being there."

"Preston Fleming? Oh, that's the fellow who's been calling. He's called here so much we'd begun to wonder if you'd started a love affair down in Caddo. First time he phoned was right after you left that Monday. There's a whole stack of messages. He's called every other day for two weeks. Just to ask if you were back and to ask you to return his message," Jasper said. "Is he someone I need to worry about?"

"He's married and I won't return his calls. An old flame that I'm having trouble extinguishing. I'll sleep three days and be ready for work on Tuesday, Jasper. Maybe by then I'll have the fire put out."

"Good luck. Just don't come in here telling me you're going off to a pig farm and giving up the job you were born to do."

"Cattle ranch, not pig farm," She said, a slow, tired smile covering her face. David had already called a taxi for her and it was waiting by the time she reached the front door. A few minutes later she opened the door to her apartment, set her suitcase down, and threw herself on the sofa. She'd forgotten about all the boxes and bags. Well, they'd have to wait because she was going to have a long, hot bath and then she was going to wallow in her own bed, right after she turned the phones off. If anyone called they could leave a message. She'd think about talking to them when she came back to the land of the living.

She shed clothing as she went to the bathroom and started a steamy bath complete with bubbles. She lit a candle and set it on the edge of the garden tub and pinned her hair up with a couple of bobby pins. She eased her tired body into the hot water and shut her eyes in appreciation. Two weeks of twenty hour days. Catching an hour of sleep here, thirty minutes there, and constant work, not to mention the fear when she looked up and saw the man she'd been profiling for nearly twelve days. But what scared her more was knowing that she couldn't get Preston off her mind. She lived in fear that he would keep her from getting the job done. Would it be like that every time she started on a new assignment?

She leaned back in the tub. The warmth relaxed her so much that she fell asleep. Two hours later she awoke to find the water chilly, the bubbles flat, a string of wax streaming down the outside of the bathtub, and her skin resembling a dried prune. She wrapped a big white towel around her body and padded into her bedroom. The door to the guest room stood wide open, and she remembered that she needed to clean out the dresser drawers. She'd do it the next day. Then there would be ten drawers to use for storing all the memorabilia she had brought back from her high school years. She threw the white, down-filled comforter back and slipped between the sheets. She was too tired to even think about hunting through her dresser drawers for a nightshirt or gown. Besides, there was no one to care if she slept for twenty-four hours in the buff.

Her head had barely carved out a comfortable spot in the pillow before she was sound asleep. She dreamed of Preston again. There was a deep fog and he walked away from her into it. She screamed his name over and over, begging him to take her with him, but he just waved without even looking back at her and disappeared into the gray mist. Kitty awoke at two o'clock in the morning. She sat straight up in bed and felt around the covers. Where was Preston? Had the fog consumed him? She was drenched in sweat. Then she remembered where she was and that she'd been dreaming. She threw herself back on the pillow and looked at the digital alarm clock beside her bed. It was dark, so that meant she hadn't really slept twenty-four hours. She had been asleep for fourteen hours, though, and now she was wide awake in the middle of the night.

Her stomach growled, reminding her that it couldn't remember the last time she'd been kind enough to think about food. She pitched back the covers and turned on the lamp on her bedside table. The answering machine was blinking like lights on a Christmas tree. She'd listen to the messages after she ate. If Jasper thought he could change his mind and make her come back Monday, he could just think again. She shuffled through the top drawer of an antique oak chest of drawers and found a pair of underpants and a T-shirt.

She went to the kitchen. There was an apple with a big bruise on one side in the refrigerator, along with a half gallon of milk that had gone bad. She did find a dozen eggs, and some onions and peppers in one drawer. There was a bag of frozen English muffins in the freezer, so she opted for a western omelet and toasted muffins. She ate every single crumb and then dug around in the pantry until she found an unopened package of Oreos. She was walking through the apartment eating them right out of the package wishing she had milk to dunk them in, when the silly dream about Preston and the fog came back to plague her. Well, good hard work could take care of that. She'd clean up the aftermath of the auction, and not think of him or that dream again.

Kitty laid the cookies on the antique wooden coffee table in her living room and opened a cardboard storage box. A stack of letters tied with a red ribbon was the first thing she pulled out. "Now what do I do with these, and why does he want me to call him? Did he find a stash of gold in the cellar on the old property and his honest conscience won't let him claim it?" She laughed at that idea.

She dumped the box of the rest of its treasures and carried it and the letters down the hall. She didn't have to throw them out right then. But she did have to clean out the dresser in order to have storage room for them. She'd use the box she'd just cleaned out to fill up with her aunt's things from the drawers, and set it beside the door to donate. Surely ten drawers would hold everything she wanted to keep.

She threw the letters on the bed and opened the first drawer. She quickly filled the box with the contents of the top two drawers. Then opened the bottom drawer where Aunt Bertha's sweaters were kept. She remembered Aunt Bertha wearing the white lacy sweater to church in the spring and fall. She crammed all eight of them in the box. The only thing left in that drawer was the envelope filled with letters from her mother all those years ago. Kitty remembered seeing her mother sitting at the little desk in the living room every Sunday afternoon, dutifully writing to Aunt Bertha, the only living relative she had left. She picked up the faded envelope and wondered why Aunt Bertha had only kept a few.

"Oh, well, I don't need to read about the day when I pulled my front tooth, or had to go to the doctor with an ear infection." Kitty tossed the envelope in the small trash can at the end of the dresser. She lugged the box of sweaters and lingerie into the living room. She sat down on the floor, crossed her legs, and ripped the duct tape from another box. She picked up a stack of pictures, one of her and Lisa in their cheerleader uniforms on the top. A white ribbon was tied around her ponytail. The last rays of the evening sun danced on Lisa's red hair. They were hugged up together and smiling. It was the last football game of their senior year. Back when things were still perfect. When Lisa was talking about marriage right out of high school to her sweetheart Jody, and back before she'd met Preston Fleming.

She made a dozen trips down the hall to the guest room before daylight. Preston's old letters were relegated to the bottom drawer. The "PF file" she called it when she pushed it shut. A finished file that she wouldn't have any reason to ever open again. That's what she did mentally when she finished a job. She filed all the information away and forgot about it, or she'd would have gone crazy in a year's time. If it worked at her job, it surely could work at home.

By mid-morning her apartment was back in order. She'd dusted, vacuumed, and plumped the cushions on the navy and ecru-striped sofa. Only one thing left to do: take out the trash.

In the guest room she picked up the trash can with the manila folder full of letters and turned it upside down in the trash bag. She thought about retrieving the letters just to see what her mother had written. Maybe she'd be sorry later that she hadn't kept them. After all, there wasn't an awful lot she had that her mother had actually written. A couple of long letters about the past might be nice.

"That's enough," she said, dragging the bag down the hallway to the kitchen. "I don't need anymore than what she wrote to me. What's in there was between her and Aunt Bertha." She wrapped a twist-tie around the top of the bag and set it outside her door on the landing. She'd take it to the big trash container at the end of the parking lot as soon as she got dressed.

She put a Lorrie Morgan CD in the player and danced around the room as she got dressed in a pair of soft, faded jeans and a button-up chambray shirt. She needed to date again. Seriously, this time. Not half-heartedly like she'd done ever since Preston had broken her heart. She stopped in the middle of a two-step and wondered again why on earth he wanted to talk to her. If he had found a million dollars worth of bearer bonds under the bathroom linoleum he could just keep it, because it would be a cold day in July when she called Preston Fleming.

The doorbell rang. She peeped out the keyhole to see Mitch, the twelve-year-old kid who lived next door, standing there with a worried expression on his face. "Hey Mitch," she said as she opened the door. "What's . . . oh, my goodness!" She exclaimed as she saw the trash bag she'd set outside the door torn to smithereens and the trash blowing all over the landing.

"There was a big dog, Stray, I guess," he said. "When I come out to get Daddy's paper he run off, but he'd sure tore up this trash. I figured you better know about it before it made a bigger mess. I'll help you clean it up."

"Thanks, Mitch," she said, and ran back to the kitchen for a couple of bags.

She handed one to the boy and the two of them began cleaning up. "Oh my, what a mess."

"Yep, but we can get it picked up in a hurry," he said.

She chased down a bunch of crumpled papers. Credit card bills. She found the manila envelope with her mother's handwriting blown all the way to the far end of the landing, practically glued to a neighbor's door.

"That's all of it," Mitch said. "I'll run the sacks

down to the big trash can for you." He held his hand out to take her sack.

"Thanks again, Mitch," she said. "I couldn't have gotten it all done without you. You're a good neighbor."

"Whoops, we missed one piece," he said as he started down the stairs. Kitty watched him pick up a letter and a flash of red caught her eye. Little red hearts. She'd recognize them anywhere. She'd put all of Preston's letters in the drawer, she was sure of it. So how did one stray letter get thrown into the trash?

"Wait a minute, Mitch." She caught him at the bottom of the steps. "What did you pick up?"

"This." He held it out.

Worry started in the center of her heart and spread outward as she turned the letter over. It wasn't addressed to her at all, but to Preston Fleming at his military address. It was the letter she'd pinned it on the mailbox for the carrier to pick up that last morning just before she left.

"Something you shouldn't have tossed out?" Mitch asked.

"That's right, and I think I'd better go through the trash again before I really get rid of it," she said. "If you don't mind toting it right back up the stairs, I'd appreciate it."

"Sure thing." Mitch smiled.

Kitty dumped everything in the two bags into the middle of her clean living room floor. She found ten more letters with heart stamps on the back of the envelopes. All addressed to her except the one. How on earth had they gotten into the trash can, though? Then a flash of the manila folder flitted across her mind. She dug through the trash, piece by piece, bit by bit. There were no letters from her mother to Aunt Bertha.

"But why did Aunt Bertha hide letters inside an envelope from Mother?" She drew her eyes down quizzically.

She looked at what she had in her hand as if the addresses might have changed in the past five minutes. No, there were ten in all. All addressed to her. All unopened . . . and all from Preston. And one from her to Preston. So he hadn't ever known how much he'd hurt her after all. Well, she sure didn't need to read love letters this late in the game. Aunt Bertha had known how bad she'd hurt and just didn't send the rest of his letters on to her in Tulsa. Kitty kept the one she'd written him and tossed the rest into the trash bag.

She put the whole stack back in the little round trash can in the guest room. It was over. He was married. She didn't need to open up old wounds again. Then before she even knew what she was doing, she reached into the can and snatched the letters all out again. She held them close to her chest and breathed deeply.

She took all of them to her bedroom and arranged them on the bed in front of her according to the dates they were mailed. She nibbled her fingernails, then forced her hands under her as she sat cross-legged, staring at the envelopes. She was asking for heartache if she read them, yet she couldn't make herself get rid of them without seeing what he'd written. Especially that last one. Did he explain why he'd found another woman? Had Tammy been the Navy woman who'd taken his heart from her?

She picked up the first one and opened it. It was dated before the phone call, and he was so much in love, it brought tears to her eyes. He remembered the way she looked as he drove away from her that final night and said he'd cried all the way back to his folks' farm. He was glad she couldn't see his tears. The second one was more of the same, and so forth until she reached the last one, tears streaming down her face, as she wondered how he could write with such passion when he was seeing another woman the whole time.

She wiped the tears away and opened the last one. Eight pages of devastation about how he felt when her aunt told him she was going back east to marry the man she'd known in the summers while visiting her father. On one page he begged her to reconsider and not go; the next he railed at her for not being honest with him. How could she write such loving letters when she was in love with another guy? If she would just please talk to him on the phone and tell him what happened, or at least write him a letter explaining the whole thing. His heart was in shambles and his mind about to join it, he said repeatedly. The ink was smudged in places where his tears had fallen on the letter, and she remembered the night she wrote the one to him. She'd left the stains on the words so he would see how much she was hurting.

She threw the letter down, still trying to find a notion of sanity amongst what she'd read. Like a bolt of lightning shooting through her veins, understanding dawned. Aunt Bertha had told them the same thing about the other one. She had never wanted Kitty to get mixed up with Preston. She'd even been downright rude to him on more than one occasion. Then, when the opportunity presented itself, she'd told him that Kitty was going back east to marry someone else. After that, she concocted a story about Preston and another woman. Before any of it could be undone, she'd died.

Now it was five years later. Five years too late, because Preston might not have had another girl then, but he sure had a wife now. It was certainly too late for Kitty Maguire to find a place in his life. All because neither of them had a chance to make things right. Aunt Bertha hadn't forwarded the letters which arrived after Kitty went to Tulsa. She had taken the one off the mailbox Kitty had pinned there before she left. So Preston didn't know anything, either.

No doubt, in her own warped mind, Aunt Bertha had thought she was saving Kitty from some fate like her own. Kitty's father, Timothy, had told her that day in the hospital about Aunt Bertha being left standing at the altar. That would have been a crushing blow to any woman's pride, especially in those days. Kitty wiped at the stiff, dried tears on her cheeks. But no matter how hard she tried, she just couldn't find forgiveness right then toward some interfering woman who'd wrecked her life.

Fate had sure played some ugly tricks on the unsuspecting. However, Kitty wasn't about to leave it alone. Not now. She fully well intended that Preston know she wasn't that kind of woman. And while she was at it, she might just waltz right up to Lisa's porch and tell her the story, too.

Chapter Eight

She drove down I-35 until she reached Ardmore, then cut through the countryside through Tishomingo, Milburn, and Kenefic on her way to Caddo. There was an outside chance she might find Preston's big gray Dodge pick-up truck at the Dairy Queen or at one of the two houses he'd just bought. They could settle the whole thing before the next day and she could get on back home without having to stay in a motel. If she knew where he lived she'd walk right up on his porch and hand-deliver the letter, but she didn't.

She could have called him on the phone, gotten his address, and mailed the letter to him. But after the way she'd been treated she wanted to see him face to face when she handed him the still unopened letter she'd written that night. It still seemed impossible that Aunt Bertha just plain lied to them both. She could fully well understand why the whole town whispered behind her back, but there was that little part of her that wanted to set them on their ear. To show them she hadn't been some kind of devil who'd played with Preston's emotions, then broke up with him while he was out to sea and couldn't do one blessed thing about it. He'd be in church tomorrow morning, and if tradition still stood, he'd be at his folks' house for Sunday dinner. She'd take the letter to him there.

She crossed under the archway in the middle of the afternoon. "Welcome to Caddo," it read. Was she truly, truly welcome in Caddo? She didn't think so. She might never be welcome again, but she wasn't going to leave town this time until Preston Fleming heard her side of the story.

She stopped at the Dairy Queen for an ice cream cone, but Preston wasn't there. Nor was he lingering around the two empty houses, so she drove on to Durant. She checked into a motel just east of the Wal-Mart where she'd seen Preston with his wife, Tammy. By the time she carried her tote bag up the stairs, she was as emotionally drained as she'd been the day before when she'd gotten off the plane in Oklahoma City. She layed on the bed for several minutes before she could control her wandering thoughts, most of which began with a single, solitary word: why?

Finally, she fished around in her purse for a phone card and picked up the receiver. She punched in all the right numbers and Timothy's voice answered on the other end.

"You got time to talk?" Kitty asked.

"Always have time to talk to my daughter." Timothy's Irish brogue filled her ears and brought with it a little comfort. "I'm off to Penn State for a consultation with some new recruits. My taxi will be here in exactly ten minutes, but I can send it on and change my flight if I need to. How'd the job in Dallas go? I called the agency and they said you were down there for a couple of weeks."

"Aunt Bertha lied to me," Kitty said bluntly. "She told Preston that I was going back east to marry some fellow I'd met there when I visited you. You already know what she told me."

"How did you find that out?" Timothy asked.

"Found some letters. She probably intended to destroy them, but then she died that next week, remember?"

"Yes, and you had surgery and couldn't go down there for the funeral. Seems like you'd better straighten out a hornet's nest," Timothy said. "You about to go back to Caddo, then?"

"I'm in a motel in Durant now. I'll see him after mass tomorrow morning. Daddy, he's married and it sure can't be undone. But I can let those good people know I wasn't the one to blame," Kitty said.

"You sure he's married?" Timothy asked.

"Saw him with his wife," Kitty said. "Right in the Wal-Mart parking lot."

"My taxi just arrived. Want me to fly into Dallas and come up to hold your hand through this?" he asked.

"No, I just needed to hear your voice. You might remember me with an Irish blessing about ten tomorrow morning. I'm going to have a confrontation with him after church."

"I'll do it." Timothy chuckled. "Lead with your left

and cross with your right if the going gets tough. I love you, Kitty Maguire."

"I love you, too, Daddy."

There, she'd said it out loud. Aunt Bertha had lied. Aunt Bertha, who had gossamer wings and a pure gold halo, who never did anything sinful in her entire life, had completely destroyed two lives. It didn't matter that she'd been left at the altar by some philandering youth when she was sixteen. Or that Katherine and Timothy had divorced. Nothing gave her an excuse to ruin Kitty's life.

She picked up the remote control and surfed through the channels until she came to the County Music Television channel and left it there. Good old solid working man's music to pass away three to five minutes at a time. Sara Evans and Vince Gill teamed up for the song "No Place That Far." The tinkly piano music at the beginning of the song made Kitty's eyes sting with fresh tears. She could relate to every line in the song when Sara sang about waking up without him being there and her world falling apart without him. Unlike the song, she couldn't swim a hundred rivers or run or crawl or even walk back into his arms. It was too late.

Five years too late.

One wife too late.

Sara mentioned two stubborn hearts in the song and nothing short of God above turning her away from his arms. It would take more than even God to put Kitty and Preston back together. She'd give him the letter and back out of his life. He might not have had a woman back then, but things had changed in five years. Neither of them were the thunderstruck young kids they had been back then. She probably wouldn't even like Preston. His ego was bigger than his belt buckle when he came to the auction, and that little stunt of tipping his hat when he caught her staring just drove the point home a little more. It was a cinch he wouldn't like her anymore since she wasn't the sweet little girl he'd met. She'd seen the other side of humanity so many times she was cynical, and when he got to know her, he'd figure that out. He'd hate her after two weeks even if they had the opportunity to get to know each other again. Which they wouldn't, because he was a married man.

At least, though, he'd realize that she hadn't broken his heart after all. Aunt Bertha had done a fine job, but Kitty had had nothing to do with it. Somewhere in the middle of Faith Hill singing "Breathe," she fell asleep. When she awoke it was dark in the room and the television was still playing one video after another. Kitty stretched all five feet, four inches of her slim body, trying to get the kinks out. She started a hot bath, added bubbles and oil, and stripped out of her clothing. She'd have to make herself go back to sleep or else she was going to have a rough time the next week. Already her schedule had been turned around. She wanted to sleep in the day or early evening and wake up at midnight or after. A couple of more days and she'd be so grouchy Jasper would send her to Siberia for a month.

Surprisingly enough, after the bath, she went right back to sleep and didn't wake up until the next morning. She dreamed about Preston and the fog again, and somewhere in the middle of it, he reappeared. In the dream she called Jasper to tell him she was going to raise pigs on a dirt farm and live in a two-room, tar paper shanty.

"That's a hoot," she exclaimed the next morning when she carefully applied her make-up for church. "I wouldn't live in Caddo even if Preston Fleming had never been married and fell down on his face and licked my toes. There's nothing in that little place for me, and like Jasper said, I was born to work for the agency. Most of the time I love it. Only time I don't is when I'm in one of those live or die situations."

She slipped on a white silk sheath dress which accented her smooth, flawless complexion. She checked her reflection in the mirror. Same old Kitty. Time and circumstances continued to change, but other than a frown, Kitty was the same. At least what could be seen in a mirror. If it could portray the inside of her heart, it might be a different picture.

She drove down a side street to University Boulevard. "How could she watch me cry like that and not break down and tell me?" she wondered. "Preston, how could you believe her?"

The same way you believed her, her conscience said. *The thought that your sweet little eighty-year-old aunt could let a lie fall from her lips was foreign to both of you.*

The church was full when she went inside. The Fleming family already claimed their three pews toward the front. She slid into a back seat and picked up a book for the responsive reading. Preston sat beside Alan again. Just like he had the last time she'd attended church. She knew the exact moment he realized she was behind him. He wiggled his neck like he was trying to ease out a crick. But it wasn't a tension knot in Preston's neck. It was a pain . . . and the pain bore the name of Kitty Maguire.

That crawling, prickly sensation began on Preston's neck about the time they began the responsive reading. Kitty Maguire was in the church, somewhere behind him. He'd bet his entire ranch on it. She hadn't bothered to return any one of his messages, and he'd left plenty of them in the past two weeks. So what was she doing back in Durant, at his church, tormenting him again? Women! He'd never understand them. He wondered just what kind of game she was playing.

She slipped out of the church as soon as services were over and was backing out of the parking lot by the time Preston made his way through the throng of people surrounding him and his family. He caught the tailgate of her pickup heading east on University, and for the first time noticed the Oklahoma tag. He berated himself for not having enough sense to notice that week it sat in front of Bertha's house.

"What you going to do about it?" Alan whispered at his elbow.

"I'm going to find out exactly where she's staying. She's brought the game to Durant, so she can just get ready to play it out to the end this time," Preston declared.

"Game?"

"I've left half a dozen messages at her work and she didn't return a single one of them. She's here, so what would you call it? It's some kind of game, Alan.

I don't understand any of it. All I know is that I can feel something in my bones that says this is coming to a head. And I'm glad. Win, lose, or draw. I'm ready to get on with my life and I can't with Kitty Maguire hanging onto my heart like a bulldog," Preston said quietly.

"I'll ride with you," Alan said. "We might as well have dinner before we begin the great hunt."

"Okay." Preston nodded. "But there ain't no 'we' to it, Brother. I'm going to find her by myself."

"You might need an army." Alan laughed as he opened the door to his brother's truck and motioned to his wife and kids that he was riding with Preston.

"Not in this war," Preston said seriously.

Kitty ate a banana split for lunch at the Braum's store. She forced the food down into her nervous stomach where a hundred butterflies fluttered around. She had to eat whether the ice cream tasted good to the butterflies or not. She'd had a bag of potato chips on the way to Caddo the day before. Other than her western omelet, that was all she'd eaten. She had to make herself eat or she'd probably faint on the Fleming front porch when she asked to speak to Preston. If the Flemings still did things like they did back when she and Preston were in love, there would be a family dinner at the farm. Or else they'd all go to some restaurant then spend the afternoon at the farm. Either way, she'd find him at the farm or she'd simply wait there for him until he arrived.

Her courage began to fail her when she turned west on Chief Road just south of Caddo. She should turn her truck around and go back to Oklahoma City. If anything was ever a foolhardy plan, this was it. She didn't have a bit of business dragging skeletons out of the closet at this late date. No matter what the cause, it couldn't be changed. If she were Tammy, she wouldn't want some old flame marching up on the porch with a letter to her husband. She sure wouldn't sit still and let him read it without saying a word.

"Not until I've said my piece. I'm not even talking myself out of delivering this letter," she said stoically and drove right up into the Fleming family's front yard. She picked the letter up from the seat beside her, but didn't have time to get out of the truck before Kate Fleming, Preston's mother, was standing beside it.

"I heard you were back in town again, Kitty. Some of the family saw you sneaking in and out of church this morning. You're not welcome here. You've caused this family enough grief for a lifetime," she said icily. "Just turn this truck around and go back to whatever rock you crawled out from under. I can't believe you'd have the nerve to come right here to my house after all you've done."

"I'm here to see Preston." Kitty shoved the door open and Kate had to jump back or get hit. "Is he in the house?"

"Kitty, I mean it. You did enough damage to our family. He's finally got his life together, and we don't want you here." Kate reached out like she was about to touch her.

"You lay a hand on me and I'll file charges." Kitty's temper flared. "I said I was seeing Preston and I'll see him, if I have to wade through every Fleming in the whole county."

"Well, you can start with me." Anna, his oldest sister, stepped off the porch. "He loved you and we trusted you. So I'll be the first one you wade through, Kitty Maguire."

"What's going on out here?" Preston threw the screen door open and stepped out in the middle of a riot in the making. The expression on his mother's face said she could chew up floor joists and spit out popsicle sticks, and Anna's face was red with pure rage.

"I came to see you," Kitty said. "Just to set an old matter straight. I don't care if they all listen to what I've got to say. You're married, so it won't matter anyway. But I'm tired of being the scapegoat for something that wasn't my fault. Everyone is ready to tar and feather me and ride me out of Caddo on a bed rail and I didn't do one thing, except fall to pieces. It took me years to get my head on straight, Preston, so I can fully well sympathize with the way you must have felt."

"What are you talking about?" Preston wasn't two feet from her, looking down at all that glorious brown hair and into those mesmerizing eyes, wanting to take her in his arms. Married? He wasn't married. Far from it.

"This." She held up a letter.

He could see the red heart stickers on the back, so it must be one of his letters. One of the many he'd faithfully written up to the last one in which he'd begged her to reconsider. So she'd kept his letters. He'd kept all of hers, too. They were in a box he'd made specially for them, and every now and then he still got them out. His whole family would put a contract out on her pretty little hide if they knew that bit of news. They thought he'd gotten over her years and years ago.

"And what does one of my old letters have to do with today?" he asked.

"This is not one of your old letters. You didn't write this one to me, Preston. I wrote this one to you. The night I came home and cried a river of tears. This one never got mailed. Aunt Bertha conveniently took it off the mailbox after I left for Tulsa that morning. The morning after you called from Trinidad. I suppose you remember that day very well?"

"Yes, ma'am," he said with a curt nod. "I remember it."

"What did you do after you talked to Aunt Bertha?" Kitty asked.

"I sat down and wrote you a letter. I poured out my whole soul in that letter."

"Well, this isn't that letter." She flipped it over so he could see that it was addressed in her handwriting. "The one you wrote is at home and I didn't get it five years ago. I just found it yesterday. Since I just read the one you wrote me . . . along with the last nine that came after I went to Tulsa . . . did you hear me?" she yelled at him, as well as the whole family who stood around looking confused. "Tulsa! Not back east, but Tulsa, where I went to school for a year. Then I went to OU, where I finished my degree. I've worked at the FBI field office in Oklahoma City since I graduated. I never did go back east or marry a man there either. Plans were changed at the last minute. Daddy got me a scholarship in Tulsa. I was going to tell you when you called that night. This morning, I found the letters hidden away in Aunt Bertha's sweater drawer. I thought it only fitting you should have the one I wrote you after you talked to her that day. She must have taken it off the mailbox and kept it since it was right there with the ones you sent me. The ones she didn't forward to me," she snapped, angry at all of them for standing there with their mouths hanging open, and at him for getting married before the misunderstanding could be cleared up. She wanted to hit someone or cry. If Anna had looked cross-eyed at her right then she would have dotted her eye.

"Why did she keep your letter?" Preston took the envelope from her hand, his fingers brushing hers and sending a shock of desire surging though his whole body.

"Because I was leaving. To go to Tulsa, not back east. She knew I hadn't told you yet and that I was going to when you called. She also realized whatever you wrote to me she could just tuck away. You sure didn't need to get that letter or you would have known we were both played for complete idiots. And all because she didn't want me to ever marry anyone, not after my parents couldn't make their marriage work."

"What did she tell you?" Preston was finally beginning to understand a little bit of what happened that day.

"That you had a change of heart. You were going to marry some girl you'd met in the Navy over your Christmas break, and that I could keep the little ring you sent me. I cried and cried, but she just told me to get on with life. Then she died the next week and I had my appendix out, so I couldn't go to her funeral and everyone thought I was terrible. I just wanted you to know what really happened. Even if it is too late. I don't intend to leave Caddo with everyone whispering behind my back that I pulled a trick like that on someone I loved so much. Good-bye, Preston. I really do wish you the best in your marriage." She hurriedly got into her truck. She kept the tears at bay until she reached the end of Chief Road and pushed the gas pedal all the way to the floor of her truck.

"It's all a lie. She's just causing a scene to save her own two-timing face," Kate declared, breaking the silence. "And why did she keep saying that you're married?"

"Her Aunt Bertha told me she was going back east to marry another man. And she told her I was getting married to another woman. It's all beginning to make sense, now. I don't think she's lying at all, and for some reason she thinks I've gotten married. Did you tell her that?" Preston asked. His heart was both heavy with the weight of what had happened, and light when he remembered her saying 'someone I loved so much.' Could she still love him even after all? Was there even a faint possibility they could start again?

"No, I did not!" She shook her head. "I asked her about her husband and she looked stunned, but I didn't mention you having a wife. I might have if I would've thought about it, just to make her go away. Explain this one more time to me, Preston. I'm beginning to feel a whole lot foolish. But Bertha Mason telling a lie? Good grief, that's as far fetched as handing out popsicles in Hades. Are you sure Kitty's not lying just to cover up her own tracks?"

"Bertha Mason told us both the same lie with only a little variation. We might have straightened it out, but the woman died, and Kitty never came back to town until a few weeks ago," Preston said. "I'm going home now, Mother. I've got a lot of thinking to do, and I want to be myself to do it."

"I guess you do," Kate said seriously. "If you talk to her again, tell her I'm sorry for what I said. Good grief, Bertha Mason doing something like that."

"Confusing, ain't it, Momma?" Preston held the letter to his heart and got into his truck. He drove away slowly, leaving them all in the yard, trying to make sense out of the way their world had been upset in less than five minutes.

Chapter Nine

Kitty reached her motel room, exasperation still tearing her apart. She threw her things haphazardly into the overnight bag and slung it in her car, pulled around to the motel office, and checked out. She'd accomplished what she'd come to Durant to do. Just as surely as when the work she loved had helped to rid society of people who committed crimes, the job was finally finished. It was time to go home. She still had Monday to relax and then she'd ask Jasper to send her to the backside of Egypt. Siberia didn't even look so ominous as she pulled out onto Highway 70 headed west. She'd catch I-35 in Ardmore and be home in three hours.

All those years she'd been three hours from Preston and could have driven down at any time, or if he'd known he could have come to Oklahoma City. If he hadn't married Tammy. She shook the thoughts from her head. She wouldn't dwell on what might have been. It would drive her absolutely crazy. She crossed the bridge across Lake Texoma and plugged a cassette into the player in her truck. Next week she was going to trade vehicles. She was going to buy a flashy little green sports car with a CD player.

Alan Jackson's voice filled the cab of the truck. Anger turned to frustration and the tears began to roll down her cheeks. Alan sang "Livin' On Love." He said that without someone, nothing wasn't worth a dime. Kitty wiped the moisture from her cheeks before it dripped onto her white silk dress. In the song, Alan mentioned two old people sitting on a porch and they were still living on love.

"I'd sit on the swing with Preston," she said aloud, her voice cracking in the middle of every word. She finally let the dam of tears loose and slapped the steering wheel when they flowed from her delicate jawbone like a river, dripping onto her white dress, leaving big circles. She wiped at them with the back of her hand, making even a bigger mess. After a few minutes she stopped even trying. The cleaners could get the water spots out. If they couldn't she'd put the dress in the drawer with the tear-stained letter Preston sent her from somewhere in the middle of nowhere.

She opened her apartment door at 4:30 in the afternoon and went straight for the phone. She dialed the familiar number and waited a moment before she hung up. In less time than it took her to walk down the hallway to her bedroom the phone rang.

"Kitty, what's wrong?" Jasper said.

"I'm in a mess. I need to talk. Can you meet me at the agency even though it's Sunday? I need to talk to someone." Her voice broke in the middle of the rush and she sobbed.

"I'm at the agency. Can you drive safely? No, don't drive. I'm sending a cab. It'll be there in five minutes. Are you okay for that long?" Jasper asked, real concern and fear in his voice.

"Probably. I just can't make it through the night," Kitty said.

"Five minutes. It'll be on your curb. Get out of the apartment and wait outside. Promise me you won't do anything stupid. Don't even go into the room where . . ."

"I'm in the bedroom where my weapon is right now," Kitty said with very little emotion left in her voice. The tears had stopped. There was nothing left but a numb spot where her heart used to be. It didn't even hurt anymore, not like that day when Aunt Bertha lied to her. Something that was dead couldn't hurt, so apparently her heart had finally died. Nothing could ever hurt it again. It would never feel again. Never know that floating sensation of being in love. Never ever feel that way again. That special way she'd known with Preston all those years ago. So why should she go on living?

"I'll pick up my purse and sit on the bench outside," she promised. Her voice resounded back to her ears and sounded like a whisper in a tunnel. Something far away and very unsure of itself. Not at all like Kitty Maguire.

She stared at the crepe myrtle bush at the end of the bench while she waited. She didn't see the pink blooms or the hummingbird flitting in and out among them. She didn't see the Monarch butterfly or the kids across the street playing on their scooters. All she saw was a funeral procession in the back of her mind. She and Jasper were going to bury the past this afternoon. A long, black limousine held the remains of Kitty Maguire's heart. She'd finally cracked and it had nothing to do with a horrible case. A simple man, an architect and rancher with a little auctioneer thrown in, had been the perp who had killed her for the second time.

The taxi was there in three minutes. She calmly climbed inside. Jasper met her at the door and put a protective arm around her shoulders. He led her to the back room, seated her in an overstuffed leather chair, and sat down behind his desk. Kitty meticulously removed her shoes and curled up in the chair, her legs under her and her face buried in her hands. She'd been in the same position once before, the first time she'd worked a crime scene and saw what a human being could do to another. She'd studied the case from top to bottom. When she began to fit the clues together, she could see the man who did it. Three days later he was behind bars, and Kitty had taken her resignation into the office. She couldn't do the job.

Jasper assured her that it wasn't unusual to feel the way she did. As a matter of fact, it was that sensitivity that made her good at what she did. She agreed to try one more time and she'd succeeded. With Jasper's help. That other day, she had lain on the sofa and didn't think anyone could ever help her again. It wasn't totally unlike the feeling she had right then, even though she was curled up in a chair rather than the sofa in his old office.

"I was hurting so bad and now I don't. I think this must be what it feels like to be dead," she simply said.

Preston carefully opened the letter and read it. She'd begged and pleaded in the letter. She'd reduced herself to humiliation and he'd never even known. He reread the ten pages twice more, then got up and packed a bag. She'd gone home to Oklahoma City, and even though her phone number was unlisted, he knew exactly what street the agency was on. He'd spend the night in a motel and tomorrow morning as soon as the doors opened he would see Kitty again.

Whether she liked it or not, they were going to talk. For a long time. Seriously. If there was no future for the two of them, then he'd have to learn to live with that. But if there was, then he intended to begin that future tomorrow morning. He left a message on the company answering machine for Alan. Then he pitched his bags into the back seat of his truck and headed west on Highway 70. By the time he reached the bridge over Lake Texoma, he was furious.

"Why?" he screamed loud enough that the echoes rattled around in the truck cab like marbles in a tin can. "Just tell me why? We didn't do anything wrong. We just fell in love and wanted to be together the rest of our lives."

Three hours later he was on the outskirts of Oklahoma City. Thirty minutes after that he found the street address for the agency. He'd already decided to check into the nearest motel, but he noticed several cars parked in the lot. Could one of them possibly be Kitty's car? She drove her pickup in and out of

Caddo, but that didn't mean it was her only vehicle. She could be inside the building. Of course, they would be locked, he thought as he stopped his truck. But someone might answer the door if he knocked.

If Kitty was in there, he'd gladly commit a felony and run his truck right through the front doors just to be able to talk to her. He smiled, the first time since he'd read the letters, at that thought. That would create quite a stir. The front end of a truck sitting in their lobby and Kitty screaming at him to drop dead.

He turned the engine off and watched the front door for fifteen minutes. "Nothing ventured, nothing gained," he said. He shook the legs of his jeans down over the tops of his boots and knocked on the door. The minutes crawled by. He knocked again, this time harder and longer. Finally a short, bald headed guy poked his head out. He would have made a wonderful Santa Claus if someone would loan him a wig and fake beard.

"You've got the wrong place, Mister. This is Sunday. You're at the FBI offices," he said.

"I'm Preston Fleming and I'm searching for Kitty Maguire." Preston looked him right in the eye and didn't back down a fraction of an inch.

"Come right in." He swung the door wide open. "Thank goodness you came by. I'm so glad to see you. Follow me."

"What's going on?" Preston stopped at the first desk. Something didn't feel right. The FBI needed him? What for?

"It's Kitty. Explaining all of this would take too long, Mr. Fleming. Are you married?"

"No sir. Never have been and not looking to be real soon." Preston shook his head.

"I'm glad. Kitty is here. She's . . ."

"She's what?" A cold dread filled Preston.

"I don't know what to say, except follow me. You two really need to talk."

"That's the first thing you've said that's made a bit of sense," Preston said. "Where is she?"

"Let me go in first. You wait by the door." Jasper didn't wait for an answer.

Kitty stared at the wall beyond Jasper's desk. She was waiting for Jasper to answer the knock on the door. Probably one of the other agents who had forgotten their keys and needed to do a bit of weekend catch-up. The last thing she'd told Jasper was that Preston Fleming had her heart in his shirt pocket and she couldn't live without it. She'd admitted that she was desperately in love with the man, but that she couldn't do a thing about it since he was married. There wasn't much more that needed saying.

"Kitty is in there. She's depressed, angry, and numb. I don't know what to do with her. But I think you do. So it's your turn." Jasper pointed toward the door.

"What do I say?" Preston asked.

"Hey, if you don't know that, then you can turn around and go home," Jasper said coldly.

She was still curled up in a ball when Preston slipped into the office. He sat down behind the desk and waited. He sat patiently for several moments, trying to form his thoughts into words, waiting for her to look up.

"Kitty?" He finally said just above a whisper.

"What are you doing here?" She bolted straight up, her eyes flashing daggers across the room at him. "Who let you in? Get out right now." She pointed toward the door.

"We are going to talk." He set his jaw and frowned.

"We're going to talk?" She laughed. "I don't think so. The time for talk is over, Preston. Five years over. One wife over."

"I'm not married. Never have been. There wasn't a Navy woman. There isn't a woman now," he said. "And we're going to talk. We're going to see if there's enough left to build another relationship on. We're going to see if the love we had could possibly still be alive. We'll see if it is as strong as it was back then. You're either going to take the rest of my heart or give me back the half you're holding. It's pretty hard to function with half a heart."

"Try doing it with no heart. I gave you all I had," she said. "But that was when we were kids. Just ignorant, innocent kids. We're adults now, Preston. You won't like me. I might not like you." She didn't make a move to cover the space between them.

"I might like you, but if I don't, I'll sure enough tell you so." He toyed with the pencil on Jasper's desk.

"Go away," she said bluntly. "I'm not taking a chance like that again."

"Okay," he said and walked out the door.

A few seconds later Jasper swung the door open. Kitty was sitting upright in a chair, her head held high and her chin thrust forward. Her shoes were on her feet and she was ready to go home. Forget mental exhaustion. Forget Preston Fleming. She was over the hump. "Send me to the far corners of the earth. India will do fine. Russia would be better. I don't care where. Just get me away."

"Sure," Jasper said. "You're a walking time bomb, lady. You aren't worth a dime to me in this condition. You're going with that tall cowboy out there. You're going home to Caddo and get your heart straightened out. Two weeks. That's how long you've got, Kitty Maguire. Come back to me whole or don't come back. I wouldn't put a BB gun in your hands right now and I sure wouldn't send you anywhere to do a job."

"I'm not going anywhere," she declared.

"That's just what I said." Jasper took a hard edge with her.

"I'm not going to Caddo." She rephrased the sentence. "I'm perfectly fine. My mind is fine now. I could shoot the eyes out of a coyote at a hundred yards. My hands are steady as an oak tree. I can do my job, Jasper." She held her hands out, palms up, to prove her point.

"Yes, they are, and yes, you could. But your sensitive heart, that place that produces the person you are, isn't so steady. You're going home with him, Kitty. I mean it," Jasper said.

She glared at him.

"Save the dirty looks," Jasper said. "You're wasting them on this old buzzard. Besides you're good enough at what you do to know yourself, Kitty. The cowboy wants to take you home, and it sounds like a good idea to me. You two have got to get this whole thing sorted out or neither of you are worth a solitary dime."

"I don't like it," she said.

"I don't care," Jasper shot right back. "He's taking you to your apartment for a bag and I don't want to see your face in here until it is straightened out. That's the bottom line, lady. Go or I'll put you on leave for six months. The only way you'll get back in is to go through extensive counseling. Twice a day for the whole six months. You going to take care of it or am I?"

"I'll do it, but I'll be back in two weeks. Not one thing will be changed. And you have to promise me a job at least a thousand miles away," she retorted. How dare Jasper treat her like a child? She was good at her job. The best he had and the youngest. She'd show him. In two weeks, she'd have everything figured out so well, Preston's name would never surface again.

"He's waiting," Jasper said. "Call me if the going gets tough."

"When the going gets tough, I get tougher," Kitty said, but she made no move toward the door. Two weeks with Preston. Where would she stay? What would they talk about? The past was over, finished, done with. The future was tomorrow. Today was what they had and it looked almighty scary.

"Well, glory, had I known the right cord, I'd have done it an hour ago," Jasper said.

Kitty glared at him. "I'll see you in a couple of weeks."

"I hope so," Jasper said when she slammed the door behind her. "I surely hope so."

Preston stood against the wall beside the front door.

She should say something to him but there were no
words, so she just stopped and stared. Two whole
weeks. Four hours ago she would have kissed Jasper's
bald head if he'd told her she could have two weeks
to spend with Preston. An unmarried Preston at that.
Now the idea frightened her worse than facing an
armed maniac.

"Are you ready?" he finally asked.

"I suppose, but we better get something straight
right here and now. This is not my idea. I don't like
it, but I'm being forced into it. And if I don't like you
I fully well intend to tell you so." Her gray eyes
flashed.

"I imagine you will, Kitty Maguire. I just imagine
you will." He opened the door for her.

She gave directions to her apartment in short,
clipped sentences, but that was the only conversation
that passed between them. Preston wondered if he'd
bitten off more than he could possibly chew. She sure
wasn't the sweet little girl he'd met that day at the
high school, but part of his heart still yearned for her.
A full-grown, sensuous woman had replaced that kid
with the big beautiful eyes. A sassy woman with a
prestigious job and a sharp tongue. Before it was all
said and done, he might very well decide he wanted
out of the deal.

Kitty folded her hands in her lap to keep from
reaching across the seat and touching his face. He'd
aged and it looked very, very good on him. She
wanted to snuggle up to his side. Touch that slight
cleft in his chin and kiss the soft spot right under his

ear that made him moan. She clutched her fingers together until they ached.

"So where is your place?" He parked where she told
him.

"I could drive my truck and then I could come and
go . . ." she started.

"You won't need it." He opened the door for her.
"Let's go get your things. If you forget something
there's a store on every street corner, so you can buy
whatever you want."

"How do I pack?" she asked when she opened the
door and went inside before him. "Jeans and T-shirts
for ranch duty? Black suits for office work? What do
you intend to do with me for two whole weeks? How
are you going to keep me from going crazy, Preston?
The only thing I know is work, and I love it."

"Pack jeans and T-shirts and take a light jacket.
Maybe a dressy outfit or two for when we go out to
eat. Like I said, we'll buy whatever else you need."
He wanted to take her in his arms and hold her. Chase
away that haunted look she kept trying to hide with
flashing anger in her eyes. It wasn't the right time.
Not then. Perhaps not in two weeks. Perhaps never.
But at the end of two weeks she would know that even
though it had been five years, he was still in love with
Kitty Maguire. Young girl. Grown woman. It didn't
matter. Her heart was the same and his heart knew it.

"You're calling the shots." She went into her bedroom.

He stood in the doorway and watched her, smiling
broadly when he saw the brown bear tossed in the
middle of the bed. He looked closer. Yes, that was the

ring he'd given her hanging around the bear's neck on a chain. So she did still care.

Confusion filled Kitty's soul as she threw clothing into a suitcase. There must be something left of the old feelings they'd shared. He was here, wasn't he? Kidnapping her for two weeks with Jasper's blessings. Probably with her father's, too, if Timothy knew what was going on. A bomb had just landed in the middle of her comfortable rut and she hardly had time to get out of it before it exploded. She'd lived in the groove so long, she didn't know if she could survive outside of it. She had two weeks to build another rut.

With Preston. Without him.

The choice terrified her so bad her hands trembled as she packed.

Chapter Ten

Preston parked the truck in the circular driveway in front of his long, low ranch style house. Before he could get around the truck to open the door for her, Kitty was already outside. "So, is this your house?" She asked simply, the first words she'd spoken in more than two hours.

"Yes, it is," he said. "Come inside. I've got to re-pack my bags before we leave."

"Where are we going?"

"We're not spending our time here, Kitty. Everyone in the family would be dropping by and we don't need that right now. We need time alone to get this all sorted out." He opened the front door and held it for her.

"Yeah, right. The only thing your family would stop by to do would be to string me up from the nearest oak tree," she said.

"No," he said with a shake of his head. "They'd be

coming in droves to apologize. Just remember, their reaction was as normal as ours. They didn't think your elderly aunt was capable of lying any more than we did," he told her.

"Where'd you get your psychology degree?" she asked flatly.

"Architecture, not psychology," he said. "Make yourself at home. I'll only be a couple of minutes. I've got to call Alan and pack a few things. Then we'll be gone."

"I have no say in where we go?"

"No, ma'am, not a single word," he said. "You're my prisoner for two whole weeks, and I intend to make the best of them."

She wandered through the living room. Warm, burled oak on the walls. A big stone fireplace across one end with a soft rug tossed on the hardwood floor in front of it. Furniture that begged to be sat on. Soft leather that she could sink into with a book and read for hours. No blinds or drapes on the floor-to-ceiling glass windows on the other end. No need for them. Nothing but rolling hills and a drooping sunset in brilliant oranges, yellow, and pinks bringing warmth and happiness right into the room.

The dining room was defined only by the fact that an antique, claw-footed oak table surrounded by matching chairs sat in the middle of a space on one side of a long bar separating the dining room and kitchen areas. Kitty ran her fingers over the durable wood. If it could talk, oh the stories it could probably tell about all it had seen and heard in the past hundred or more years.

Peace. A sudden peace filled her heart and soul. Something she hadn't known since the day her mother told her she was very sick and that plans had been made for her to live with Aunt Bertha in Caddo. She wasn't even aware that her peace had disappeared. Not until that very moment when she stood in the middle of a strange ranch house and listened to Preston Fleming whistling somewhere down a long hallway.

Preston dialed his brother's home number and waited while one of his nieces went outside to call Alan to the phone. Had it really just been this morning in church that an odd feeling had overpowered him when he realized Kitty was in the building with him? How could so much happen in so short a time?

"Hmmph," he snorted. Bertha Mason had destroyed his life in far less time than that. She'd done it in less than three minutes.

"Hello." Alan was out of breath.

"I'm going to take my two weeks' vacation starting right now. You can run the business without me. The Willobys aren't ready for their plans just yet, and the other construction sites don't need my daily inspections," Preston said.

"Got anything to do with Kitty Maguire?" Alan chuckled.

"Just everything," Preston told him.

"Have a good time, then. Two weeks. That's all any of us get. Remember, just because you're the architect doesn't mean you can ask for another week. It's set up in the company constitution," Alan teased.

"Thanks," Preston said softly. "I'll call in occasionally."

Kitty stood with her back to the cold stones surrounding the fireplace, watching the sunset when he walked down the hallway into the living room. For just a fleeting moment, Preston truly wondered if he was about to embark upon the right thing. Or if he should simply take her back to Oklahoma City and proceed with the whole affair in a much slower way. Jasper said he wouldn't let her work for weeks, maybe months, with her present mindset, so he'd have time to court her proper. With roses, champagne, dates.

"Lovely, isn't it?" he said.

"The most beautiful I've ever seen. Where are we going, Preston?"

"As in us or as in this trip?"

"Both." She looked right at him, her gray eyes the color of dense fog. He actually liked her better when she was angry. When she hated him. The opposite of love wasn't hate, though. It was indifference, and she looked indifferent to the whole world, him included, at that moment. The battle before him might be long and tough, but if he won Kitty in the end, it would be worth it.

"As in us, I don't know, Kitty. I just know that what I felt for you all those years ago isn't dead. I never thought I'd have the opportunity to feel that way again, and suddenly it's here and I don't know what to do with it. Or you, either. I just know that fate has handed us two weeks to see if we still have a foundation left to build on. As in this trip, we're going to Destin, Florida. On the west end of the beach is a motel I like. Sometimes I go there just for a weekend to lie on the sand and do nothing. It's a good place for us to find out if either of us can feel that way again. No relatives. No acquaintances. Just lots of pure white sand, sun, and time."

"Flying or driving?" she asked.

"Driving to Dallas. We'll stay at a hotel and I'll make plane reservations for tomorrow morning." His arms itched to hold her, but he kept a safe distance all the way across the living room.

"Ready as I'll ever be." She shrugged her shoulders. "I didn't bring a bathing suit."

"They sell them on the strip." He picked up his bag and followed her out the front door.

The moon and stars were sparkling in a dark sky when they checked into the motel room. Preston arranged for two rooms with connecting doors and disappeared into his room after he set her bags on the floor. Kitty flopped down on the bed and laced her hands behind her head and stared at the stripes on the ceiling. Light from the parking lot filtered around the edges of the drapes on the hotel window and made three perfect stripes on the ceiling. She could hear Preston's voice through the wall. He must be making plane reservations. Two weeks in Florida. There wasn't a thing this side of the moon she wouldn't have given last week for an opportunity like this. Fourteen days with no puzzles to put together. What was it Preston said? Nothing but time, sun, and white sand.

"Yeah, right," she whispered. "No puzzles as in profiling some criminal. But the puzzle in my heart would make that kind of work look like child's play."

She hadn't had time like that in five years. From

the day she walked out of Aunt Bertha's house, she'd kept busy to chase away the pain. She crossed her eyes and made six stripes on the ceiling. Sun . . . that was a crazy idea. If she layed out until six days past eternity she still wouldn't tan. She might burn and peel, but her buttermilk-white skin did not tan. White sand? She wiggled her toes just thinking about sinking them deep into it.

The door opened, the light erasing all the stripes on her ceiling. How dare he not even knock? She bit her lower lip and set her jaw in anger. *Good grief*, she scolded herself. *If everything he does for two weeks makes me mad, we'll never get anything settled.*

"Are you asleep?" he whispered.

"No," she whispered back. "But I'm hungry. Did you bring me to Dallas to starve me to death or does the prisoner get to go out for supper?"

"I thought we'd order something from the restaurant downstairs and have it delivered." He sat down on the edge of the bed.

"Okay. When is the prisoner to be trusted? Can she take a shower alone?"

"I don't know," he grinned. "Maybe not. I might need to call Jasper and see if she's ever escaped by crawling through the drain pipe. He says she has so many tricks up her sleeve I'd better be extra careful."

Kitty snorted and almost smiled. "I'm not that skinny," she retorted.

"I didn't say you were." He started at her feet and let his eyes slowly travel upward to her face. "I think you are put together right well, Kitty Maguire."

"Oh, hush." She sat up and switched on the lamp

beside her bed. "I want a steak. Medium rare. T-bone
if they've got it. KC strip if they don't. I could settle
for a sirloin but it's not my first choice. Baked potato.
Extra butter, sour cream. Topped with grated Monte-
rey jack cheese and chopped black olives. Salad with
honey mustard dressing, and if they have decent
homemade bread, I'll have a half a loaf of that. Sweet
tea. A whole pitcher with no lemon."

"Yes, ma'am." He picked up her phone. He relayed
her wishes without missing a single olive, then told
them to double the order. "Twenty minutes." He said
when he laid the receiver down. "Take your shower
and I'll see what's on television. Maybe we can catch
one of those pay-per-view movies."

"I get to shower all by myself?" She opened her
bag and took out the things she needed.

"If you want company . . ." He laid the remote down
on the bed.

"Oh, no," she said. "You stay in here. There's not
even a window in the bathroom or a ceiling vent. You
don't have to worry about me escaping."

"How do you know all that?" he asked.

"I already checked it out," she said flippantly and
disappeared into the bathroom.

She dropped her jeans and T-shirt on the floor and
turned on the hot water. She sat down on the edge of
the tub and added cold water until it was just under
the steaming point. She had fifteen minutes for a soak.
Many times she would have given half her paycheck
for a quick shower. What she would've given for a
real bath couldn't be measured in dollars and cents.
She shucked out of the rest of her clothing and gasped

when she slid down into the water. It was absolutely wonderful. She freed her mind of everything for a few minutes. No work. No stress. No Preston. No trip. Just a few minutes of absolute freedom.

"Hey, Kitty?" Preston's voice jerked her out of a semi-doze and back into reality. "Are you still in there?" He sounded worried. She smiled, thinking how easy it really would be to get away from him if she wanted to. Maybe she'd do it, to show him she wasn't anyone's prisoner for very long.

"I'm here. My bottom is too fat to fit down the drain pipe," she called out. "Is supper here?"

"In five minutes," he said.

"I'll be out soon," she said. The water had cooled faster than she'd thought it could and she shivered when she stood up. She wrapped a towel around her body and rubbed all the moisture away before she stepped into a pair of cotton bikini underpants. She pulled on a pair of soft, light green, faded jersey knit pajama bottoms and a matching spaghetti-strap tank top. She turned the handle to open the bathroom door at the same time someone rapped a rat-a-tat-tat on the outer door. Without so much as a squeak of the hinges or a sigh, she peeped through a crack. Preston helped the boy roll the table into the room and shuffled through his wallet for a tip. His back was to her. It was now or never. If she was really, truly a prisoner, she wouldn't even hesitate, so why did she think twice about slipping past him and walking out the door?

She shrugged her shoulders and was in the hallway before Preston handed the waiter a bill. She'd show him exactly how far the prisoner idea was going to last. If they were going to accomplish one thing on this trip, they'd might as well get on the right foot. Beginning with him trusting her. She wasn't anyone's prisoner, even if Jasper did say she wasn't worth a dime until she got her personal life straightened out.

The elevator was right around the corner from their rooms and she was in it before the red-haired kid from the restaurant could put the money Preston handed him in his pocket. When the elevator reached the ground floor and the doors squeaked open, she smiled brightly at the people going inside. "Good evening," she said. "Would you know where I could buy the evening paper?"

One elderly gentleman cleared his throat and blushed. "Right over there, ma'am." He grinned and pointed toward a rack beside the front door.

"Thank you, sir." She nodded and padded off in her bare feet in that direction. She didn't even stop to look at the newspaper rack. Right then she didn't care about the headlines proclaiming that there was a drought in north central Texas and the governor had issued a burn ban. She'd just asked the man where to buy a paper so he would tell Preston. If she had it figured right, Preston would storm out of the room just about the same time the elevator made it to the top floor. When he asked if anyone had seen her, the elderly man would nod and tell him she had wanted a paper.

She opened the front door of the hotel and climbed into the first yellow cab in the long line. "Take me around the block, please, and bring me right back here."

"Do what?" The man asked with a definite East Indian accent.

"Around the block one time. When we get back there will be a tall cowboy standing in the front of the hotel looking a bit angry. He will pay for my ride," she said.

"Sure, lady." He nodded. It was all the same to him, whether he took her to a shopping mall or back to the hotel, but he wondered what kind of strange games she and this cowboy were playing.

Preston looked under the silver dome at the baked potatoes. Lots of black olives and white cheese. He'd never eaten them just like that but he had to admit, they sure smelled scrumptious. "Kitty, are you going to take all day in there? Food is going to get cold," he shouted toward the bathroom door.

Something wasn't right. It was too quiet. He knocked on the door and waited. "Kitty?" he yelled a little louder. Nothing. He tried the knob. Unlocked. For a split second he hesitated, then threw the door wide open. Empty. He turned quickly, but she wasn't in the room. Kitty Maguire, Jasper had said, was capable of anything. He looked up to see if there was a vent she might have used to escape. Her clothing was on the floor in a heap but she hadn't passed him, and she would have had to do so to get out of the room. He retraced his footsteps to the place where the boy had stood when he gave him a tip.

"Good grief," he moaned. "She slipped out behind us and I didn't even see her." He grabbed the key card and ran out into the hallway. He punched the button for the elevator and it opened immediately. Several elderly folks bustled out.

"Did you see a woman? About this tall?" He measured up to the middle of his chest. "Dark hair with some red highlights, gray eyes . . ."

"And pretty as a picture?" One bald-headed fellow grinned. "Wearin' a pair of green pajama things and no shoes. Asked where she could buy a newspaper. I showed her the racks and she thanked me. Mister, if I had a woman that pretty I wouldn't let her out of my sight. You better get in this elevator and go on down there. What'd you ever do to make her mad anyway?"

"I didn't do anything," Preston stammered.

"Must have. If you didn't do nothing, she'd be in the room with you, not buying a newspaper. If I had a woman like that she wouldn't be thinking about reading no newspaper," the man said.

Preston's nod was so forlorn the man roared, a big laugh from the bottom of his belly overhanging a big cowboy belt. Preston listened to him guffaw all the way down the hall as he stepped inside the vacant elevator, pushed the ground floor button, and waited impatiently for the doors to shut.

He scanned all the sofas and easy chairs in the lobby. Several people were indeed reading newspapers or magazines or watching a golf match on the big screen television set in the corner, but no Kitty. He checked behind the tall potted trees growing toward the skylights, but still no woman in green pajamas and bare feet. Finally he went outside and asked the valet if he'd seen anyone . . . just this tall with dark hair and gray eyes. Before the kid could answer, a yellow cab pulled up in front of the hotel and Kitty crawled out of the back seat. She held her head high and acted like the Queen of Sheba herself.

"Pay the man, darlin'." She smiled. "I don't think it will be too high but tip him well. He's a good driver."

"What in the devil . . ." Preston's eyes flashed pure anger.

"Just pay him. I'm starving to death. My supper is getting cold." She tossed her head to one side.

Preston pulled out his wallet and handed the cab driver a bill. "Keep the change," he said. "Now do you want to tell me exactly what this is all about?" He turned on Kitty just as she pranced barefoot through the door the valet held open for her.

"Sure." She covered a yawn with the back of her hand. "While we eat, I'll tell you all about it. Did they have a T-bone? It's been hours since I've had real food and I'm hungry enough to eat the left haunch of an Angus bull. Stairs or elevator?"

"Elevator," he said between clenched teeth.

"Scared you, didn't I?" she said when they were riding upward.

"No, more like made me furious." His jaw muscles were working overtime.

"Good," she said. "Then we're in the same frame of mind."

He used the key card to get them back into the room. She calmly walked over to the table and seated herself in a chair, put the white dinner napkin on her lap and uncovered the dishes. She sipped her tea and nodded approval.

"Now what was that all about?" He grimaced as he followed her movements.

"It was to show you that I'm not a prisoner. You couldn't keep me confined two seconds if I wanted to leave. It was to reassure me that I'm an important person and you are not my master. It was to set us on firmer ground. I'm an adult woman, Preston. I hold down a very prestigious job. And I'm good at it. I could have been at the airport by now and on a flight to Italy or Alaska or Omaha, Nebraska. Anywhere." She poked her fork at him with every word.

"Okay." He breathed out heavily. "In your bare feet? You'd go to Omaha in your bare feet?"

"If I needed to escape, I'd go in my underwear," she told him.

"How would you pay for it?"

She pulled a silver credit card from the pocket of her pajama bottoms. "There's enough money on this to buy a house on the coast in California. I don't even brush my teeth without knowing exactly where I could find it."

"Don't tell me when the bad boys catch you they always say, 'Miss Kitty, you keep this card now so in case you get away from us, you'll be able to get home.' Come on Kitty, that's pretty childish and feeble. Besides, if you have all that, why did you make me pay for the cab?" He gritted his teeth even tighter.

"It was a cheap lesson, Preston Fleming. So far the bad boys haven't found my plastic when they've caught me. Matter of fact, only one time has anyone ever been so lucky as to trap me. Now are we going to eat or argue?"

"I still think it was a childish stunt," he said shortly.

"Maybe, but it sure made me feel better." She smiled so cheerfully that her gray eyes twinkled. "I feel like I'm back in control of my own life again and that's important to me. I haven't felt this good in a long time."

"Well, remind me to let you play your little games whenever you want," he said sarcastically.

"Oh, I will, darlin'. Only I won't remind you. I'll just play them, whenever I want, however I want and as long as I want." She cut into her steak. Pink in the middle. Perfect, and she was starving. She popped a chunk in her mouth and rolled her eyes toward the ceiling. She couldn't begin to remember the last time food tasted so good.

"Kitty, we've just flat got off on the wrong foot," he said, biting into his steak. Not nearly as good as the ones from his own beef that he grilled in his own back yard, but not bad for room service in a hotel.

"Maybe," she said. "But we're right on key now, Preston. I told you I wasn't that same lovesick little teenager, didn't I? Well, I'm not. You aren't going to like Kitty the woman as well as you did Kitty the kid. Did you find a movie for us to watch while I was taking a bath?"

"No, nothing good tonight. It's late anyway and our flight leaves at eight o'clock in the morning, so we'll have to be up early. And don't tell me what I will like and what I won't. I can make up my own mind." He looked at her with the raw edges of his frustrations and anger flaring. He longed to reach across the table and take her hand in his, but she'd probably slap him into next week. Kitty the woman vs. Kitty the kid. He wondered who would win the fight and if he'd even care by the time he got back to Caddo.

She leaned back in her chair, dabbed her mouth with the napkin and tossed it on her plate. Preston trimmed the fat from his steak with the preciseness of a surgeon. Great Scott but he was good-looking. Too handsome for words, actually. She wanted to run the tips of her fingers across that sexy five o'clock shadow on his strong square chin, but more than likely if she reached across the table toward him, he'd hightail it away from her so fast she'd wonder if he'd ever been in the same room with her.

He chewed the last bite of steak slowly. "Are you finished?" he asked coolly.

She nodded. Boy, he'd never gotten that riled when they were kids and in love. But then she'd never pushed him into a white hot rage back then. It could be a long two weeks if he didn't soften up, but then it might be a profitable time even if he didn't. She would never commit her life to someone as domineering as he had been all day long. She wasn't cut out to be a docile housewife who kept her eyes on the floor and stayed two feet behind her husband. He could take her like she was or they'd shake hands like two adults and walk away from the two-week folly with nothing but sand, sun, and time wasted.

He politely pushed the table out into the hallway. "I'm going to take my shower and go to bed. I'll have the front desk give us a wake-up call at four. Breakfast is served on the flight, but with these new regulations we have to be there three hours early. We're not far from the airport so be ready to leave by four-thirty."

"Four forty-five," she challenged. "Any Texas cab driver can get us there in ten minutes. I know exactly how far it is and I could spit into a west wind and hit the terminal from here."

"Four-thirty." He started across the room.

She smiled wickedly. "I'm leaving at four forty-five. You going without me?"

"Kitty," he moaned. Were they going to have a battle of wills every time they went anywhere?

"Compromise. Four thirty-seven and I'll have my hair combed, my bags ready and the whole nine yards," she said.

"Okay," he agreed.

"Thank you." She took two steps forward, slipped her arms around his neck and tip-toed to meet his mouth as she pulled his face toward hers. Their lips met in a fierce kiss that defied all challenges. Two souls found the other half of what they'd lost five years before.

She finally pulled away and took two steps back, her hands held firmly behind her back. One more kiss like that and she'd be walking two steps behind him, casting her eyes toward the carpet and groveling at his feet for more. "Good night, Preston. And I'm not your prisoner. I'm here because I want to be. If I don't want to be at any time, I'll be gone."

"Good night, Kitty." He found his voice hiding somewhere down deep in his chest. Good grief, if seven minutes could bring on that kind of response

he'd grant her five or six hours of compromise anytime she wanted it.

He shut the door between the two rooms very gently. Everything in his body longed to reopen it and
take her in his arms one more time to see if that kiss
was real. Everything in his mind told him to take a
nice long, cold shower and not test his luck.

Kitty threw herself backwards on the bed. A door
separating two bedrooms. One simple little lock she
could pick in two minutes. She wanted just one more
of those passionate kisses to take to dreamland with
her. Her heart told her she'd better shut her eyes and
go to sleep. She'd already tested his patience to the
breaking point for one night.

Kitty didn't open the door but it was a long, long
time before she went to sleep.

Chapter Eleven

The dressing room had mirrors on three sides and Kitty didn't like what she saw in any one of them. She was five pounds too thin by her own standards. Even in the bright red and turquoise horizontal striped bikini she needed a few more pounds. "So much for never having too much money or being too thin." She fumed at her reflection. She couldn't remember the last time she cared about her appearance in a bathing suit. It must have been that summer when she had been in love with Preston and their future lay before them like a bright shining star. Only that year, she'd worried about being five pounds too heavy. Too fat. Too thin. What upset her more than anything was the fact that it affected her at all.

She touched the dark circles under her eyes that even make-up couldn't cover that morning before they had left Dallas. She'd slept very little the night before. She had to keep reminding her run a way heart that she was a different person than she was back then. She was a woman with a mind of her own. A top-notch profiler for the FBI. She'd carved out her own reputation in a rock-hard job, and she'd made a nice, comfortable personal rut for herself to live in when she left work. She didn't need Preston Fleming anymore.

Then why are you sleeping like a sugared-up, hormonal teenager at a slumber party? She asked herself. *You are tossing and turning and reliving every wonderful emotion that one impromptu kiss brought about when you could be snoring.* She shut her eyes tightly, but all she saw was the up close and very personal look on his face when she wrapped her arms around his neck and kissed him. And all she felt was that tingling down deep inside her, reminding her she was a woman who wanted a man to fulfill her life. Not just any man, either. She needed and wanted Preston Fleming, and she was terrified that when he got to know her his little bubble would burst in thin air. Or that she'd find the man she knew five years before wasn't the same one standing outside the dressing room waiting for her. She'd be left holding nothing but a two week heartache. It was better to condition herself for the worst, to strap down her dancing heart in the cold hard chains of reality, and to remind her racing thoughts that "happy ever after" never happened in real life.

"Did you find one?" he asked when she swung open the doors.

"I suppose it's as good as any." She held up a handful of brightly colored material and he raised an eyebrow. "What?" She cocked her head to one side and challenged him with the single word.

"Not a thing." He shook his head. "Just picturing you laying in the sand in that. I'll have to put lots and lots of sunblock on all that white skin or you'll be a lobster by nightfall. I seem to remember that you don't tan well."

She just nodded. She seemed to remember, with a delightful shiver, the way his hands had felt on her bare skin. The bikini hadn't been so skimpy that summer. Aunt Bertha could barely tolerate the orange one Kitty wore back then. She would have sent her to a convent, and she wasn't even Catholic, if she'd seen the turquoise and red one Kitty laid on the counter that day. But, if Aunt Bertha hadn't taken matters in her hands that year, then today wouldn't be necessary. The unsettling ideas caused Kitty to shake her head slightly.

"Change your mind?" the sales clerk asked.

"No, just shaking a bunch of errant thoughts from my head," Kitty said honestly. "I guess I need a few days on the beach."

"Don't we all." The lady smiled. "Have a good time. At least the tourist season is over and the beaches should be fairly well deserted. Weekends still get pretty hectic, but this time of week is nice." She handed Kitty the bag. "On your honeymoon?"

Kitty blushed and Preston smiled. "Of course," he said. "Two whole weeks of sun, sand, and time."

"You make a lovely couple."

"Why did you say that?" Kitty asked when they

were inside the rental car. "We aren't on our honey-moon."

"Easier. She would have blushed red as fire and we'd had to explain, so it was just easier to agree," he said as he drove toward the motel. She let that soak in while he nosed the car into the right slot for their rooms. "Meet you on the beach in five minutes?"

"Ten," she said.

"Seven and a half and one kiss to seal it?" He raised an eyebrow and she giggled. Her laughter thrilled his soul. It was rich and deep, reserved for honest joy, not an affected chuckle. Kitty was startled, herself. She hadn't felt like that in so long, she'd practically for-gotten how good a common old giggle could feel.

"Seven and a half and I'll take that kiss to seal the deal." She leaned across the seat. Mouth met mouth without any other part of their bodies touching. The sky went up in a flame of brilliant colors and she swore she heard train whistles somewhere out there in the ocean.

"Sure you want to go to the beach at all?" he asked hoarsely when she pulled away.

"Seven minutes now and it'll take that long to get those two little rubber bands they call a bathing suit pulled up on my body," she said with a giggle and a dash out of the car toward her room.

"Thirty seconds early," she said flippantly as she spread out a towel beside him and laid down on her stomach a few minutes later. "I think you said some-thing about rubbing this stuff on my back for me." She tossed a tube of sunblock toward him.

"Yes, I did." He caught it mid-air and sat up. Sexy,

dark hair covered his chest. Kitty locked her hands together over her head to keep from reaching out and tangling her fingers in the soft nest.

He squirted out a palmful of white lotion and began to massage it across her mid-section. Fire and ice, all combined in one sensation. Goosebumps rose up on her arms and every single hair on her head tingled. Her toes curled in defense against the passion flooding every cell in her body. A small moan escaped through her clenched teeth.

"Feel good, does it?" His mouth was so close to her neck that she felt his soft, warm breath. That alone set off a whole new ripple of heat. "I'll get your neck now and then your arms and backs of your legs." The tone of his voice teased but his mouth didn't drop another two inches and claim another kiss.

His fingertips prickled from touching her bare skin and his hands quivered. A trembling desire filled his insides. He wondered how in the world she could lay there as cool as a summer cucumber salad without even wiggling. She surely must not feel the same way he did, which was magnified at least a thousand percent over the time when they were just kids and freshly in love. He smeared white lotion down the backs of her muscular legs and with long sweeping strokes, rubbed it in. When he reached her toes, he had to uncurl them to get between them and on top of her instep. So she wasn't quite as cold as he'd thought. His touch affected her somewhat or her toes wouldn't be so tense.

Preston grinned ever so slightly, then eased himself back on the towel. He slipped his sunglasses back on and enjoyed the warmth of the midafternoon sun as it beat down upon his chest. "When you bake that side for half an hour, then it's my turn for you to get my back," he reminded her when he could trust his voice to speak without panting.

"Deal," she said. She'd almost moaned in ecstasy when the tips of his fingers touched her skin. Great balls of fire. She'd embarrass herself for sure when it was her turn to return the favor. But then, perhaps, it would be poetic justice. He could lay there and she could make goosebumps the size of Mt. Everest raise up on his arms when she rubbed him with sunblock. She hoped his insides were nothing more than a bowl of trembling nerves when she finished.

"Are we going to talk?" she asked without opening her eyes.

"Tomorrow maybe," he said just above a sexy, masculine whisper. "Today we are going to unwind and think about nothing."

Yeah, right, she thought. *I've had trouble keeping my mind off you for all these years and you are less than a foot away and you want me to think of nothing. You'd have to shoot me dead for me to think of nothing right now.*

"Okay," she said. "I'm taking a nice long nap in this wonderful, warm sun then. Wake me when I've got this side grilled to medium rare."

"Mmmmm," he mumbled and pretended to be already asleep. But Preston couldn't have slept. Every nerve in his body was begging to touch Kitty Maguire. His mouth wanted to kiss her. He wanted to listen to the soft sound of her voice. His body wanted to snuggle close to her side just to reassure himself that she was really there. Really flesh and blood and warm Kitty, not just an apparition.

Kitty shut her eyes tightly, sighed once and miraculously went to sleep.

"Hey, sleepyhead, time to turn over and baste the other side." Preston touched her arm and her eyelids snapped open immediately. "Besides it's your turn . . ." He held out the sunblock.

She took it from his hands and edged close enough to reach his back. She braced herself for the shock of his skin against the tips of her fingers. She was not disappointed. A solid jolt of electric desire filled her and she bit her tongue to keep from groaning out loud. She only hoped his heart was doing some kind of jitterbug just like hers. She couldn't be sure that he was even awake.

Preston deliberately concentrated on breathing. One, two, three, inhale. Four, five, six, exhale and wait to the count of three to suck more ocean air back into his lungs. Anything to keep from tackling Kitty and dragging her down beside him. He'd never make it two weeks at this rate. Another day of her hands on his back and he'd be crazy with desire. Another day, nothing! He'd already passed that stage.

"So you live alone out there at the ranch? No Blue Heelers? No Blue Tick coon dogs or anything?" she asked, trying to make small talk to rein in the desire warming up her body hotter than the sun.

"Nope," he said. "Why? You like Blue Heelers?"

"Just wondered," she said.

"Strange you should ask. I got one ordered. Alan's

dog is a crackerjack cow dog. She's going to have puppies any day now, and I've asked to pick out of the litter first. So I'll have one in about six weeks." He was glad for idle conversation.

She finished rubbing lotion on his back and squeezed a palmful of lotion into her hand and applied it to the front sides of her legs, then her flat stomach and shoulders.

He watched, mesmerized, wishing he could touch her again.

"Male or female?" she asked.

"Probably female, they're more stable. At least after they've had a liter. If I choose a female, we'll breed her back with one of Alan's studs, then I'll have her spayed. I'm not going into the business of raising dogs. But I would like one like Alan's Lady. Boy, she's one more smart cow dog." He laid his sunglasses to one side and really looked at Kitty.

"What are you going to name your new dog? Lady?"

"No, if I choose a female, which I plan on doing, I'm registering her as Madam Elisabeth Gray Eyes. I'll call her Bess though." He said. "You sure you don't like Blue Heelers?"

"Not really. I just like puppies. I don't care if they're pedigreed or not. Mother never wanted animals around. Said they were a nuisance, but I had a little friend down the block who had an old momma cat who had kittens two or three times a year, and a mongrel dog which produced the ugliest puppies in the universe. But I loved them all," Kitty said.

"So maybe you'll like Bess?" he asked. She'd actually talked about something, like she used to do back before Aunt Bertha ripped up their world.

"I don't know. I'd have to be around to see her, wouldn't I? Who knows what might happen. Preston, we're not kids. We're adults. We traveled different roads when we were torn apart. The love we had then died," she said.

"What if you met me at a party." His eyes locked with hers and held. "If we'd never seen each other before. If we had no history. No Aunt Bertha to lie to us. No mutual friends. Just me and you in a whole crowd of people. And you looked across the room and I was staring at you and I held up a glass in a toast. What would you do if I crossed the room and introduced myself?"

She didn't blink. "There's never been a doubt about our physical attraction, Preston. It was there in the beginning and we haven't changed our outward appearance so very much."

"What would you do?" he asked again.

"I'd introduce myself right back and accept the dinner invitation which you would issue on the spot. We'd leave the party and go somewhere quiet and talk until the wee hours of the morning," she said.

"Then forget the past. All of it. Forget Aunt Bertha's meddling ways. Forget the pain and heartache. And we'll go somewhere quiet and talk," he said, his blue eyes twinkling brightly.

"You're not going to like me," she said staunchly.

"Are you going to like me?" he asked.

"Who knows? I guess we've got two weeks to find

out," she answered. "Will Bess be born before we get back to Caddo?"

"Why the interest in the dog? Is it just something to talk about so we don't have to face the real issues of our hearts?"

"Maybe, I just wondered. I haven't held a puppy in a long time."

Preston would never understand her. She wanted to talk about a dog that hadn't even been born yet instead of what was really on her mind.

"I'm getting hungry. What are we doing for supper? Do I have to dress up?"

"Not tonight. We're buying fresh shrimp at the fish market. I'm making scampi in the room. I asked for a room with a kitchenette so we wouldn't have to go out every night. You can toss the salad," he said.

"What if I don't like scampi?" she asked.

"You don't? We could have steak then, or grilled chicken." He opened his eyes to find her staring unabashedly at him.

"I love scampi. With lots of slivered garlic and served up on a bed of steamed rice. I was just seeing what you'd say if I didn't like it."

"Then, let's get dressed and go find some shrimp. You've made me hungry just thinking about it. Besides, the sun is falling behind the horizon and we aren't getting a tan anyway."

"Hey, Preston," she said when they reached their rooms. "Thanks for getting two separate rooms. Without a connecting door."

"You're not a prisoner anymore, Kitty." He laid his hand on her shoulder. "You can stay or go at your own will. If you're in that room every morning when I knock, then I'll know you want to be with me for the day. If you're gone, then I'll know you went home and it's probably over."

"Thank you." She laid her hand on his and squeezed his knuckles. "Same goes for you, you know. If you decide this is more than you want to invest your vacation in, you can go home, too."

"Ain't likely." He brushed a kiss across her forehead. "I'll wait for you right here." He nodded toward a couple of lawn chairs on the concrete patio in front of their rooms. "We'll shop and then cook together." His mouth yearned for a real kiss but he wouldn't pressure her.

"I'll be right out." She disappeared inside her room. She shut the door and slid down until she was sitting on the floor. Two weeks of suppressing her raging hormones and she'd be ready for therapy twice a day for the six months Jasper threatened her with.

What would you do if we'd never met before? His words came back to haunt her as she took several deep breaths and tried to steady her jelly-filled knees.

"But we have," she whispered. "We have, and I loved you then so much it hurt. I thought I couldn't love anyone more than I did back then. I was wrong. I love you even more today. But I love my job, and they won't mix. I can't do my work without a clear head and I can't have that with you. Every thought, every breath of air, every thing I see has Preston Fleming written on it, and I don't know if I want it bad enough to give up everything else I have for it. Mother and Daddy tried the married life and it didn't work.

She found out she wanted her freedom, her life without encumbrances. Will I be like that? This has to be more than a passing fancy, Preston. Because the cost is too great."

Kitty pulled herself up and slipped out of the bikini. She took a fast shower and put on a pair of khaki walking shorts, a deep forest green knit shirt and a pair of soft leather sandals. Nothing flashy or sexy. They'd be cooking in close quarters. She'd have to keep her defenses up or else she'd succumb to the desires of her heart and forget about the future.

Chapter Twelve

"Excuse me," Kitty said for what seemed like the hundredth time since she and Preston had begun the exercise in endurance. They'd shelled the shrimp, found a skillet in the cabinet and melted butter in the first step of scampi, and every time she moved, she bumped into Preston. It was a wonder the whole kitchen wasn't a kaleidoscope of brilliant flashing lights, as sparks danced when her hand brushed against his. Or worse yet, when he turned quickly and she found herself plastered against his chest.

Preston grinned. For one time in his life he didn't mind the cramped quarters of a tiny motel kitchenette. He only hoped that every time they accidentally touched, her toes curled up as tightly as they had been when he rubbed lotion on her that afternoon.

"I think I can finish up here if you'll find us a couple of plates and set the table. There's a candle in the bag on the bed. I bought one of those big, fat ones with three wicks," he explained while he sautéed the shrimp. "Oops, I forgot matches."

"Right here." She picked up a box from a basket on the cabinet. "Evidently we aren't the first folks who forgot to bring our own fire."

Shrimp and candles, she bit back a groan. *Lord, help me*, she prayed earnestly. A king-sized bed within jumping distance from the tiny table for two, a body aching with desire, and Preston Fleming across the table from her. His blue eyes flashed back the candle flames every time she looked up. If she was truly as smart as Jasper thought, she'd march herself right out of the motel suite at that very moment. She'd pack her bags and call a taxi and never look back.

"Now turn out the lights," he said when the candle was burning brightly, "and I will serve up our supper."

She held her hands tightly in her lap, trying desperately to squeeze them so hard they'd stop shaking. Her breath caught somewhere between a gasp and a moan when Preston exhaled on her neck as he heaped rice and shrimp onto her plate. She hoped she covered it well with a cough. "Delicious," she muttered after the first bite. "You should sell your business and buy a restaurant."

"Folks would get tired of scampi." He smiled and her will power melted. "That and a mean grilled steak is the extent of my gourmet abilities. So unless you've got some hidden talents in this microscopic kitchen, then I suppose we'll be eating out on the third night of our vacation."

"I can make bologna sandwiches that are out of this world," she teased.

"With mustard and tomatoes and lettuce and dill pickles?" He raised an eyebrow and she shut her eyes, pretending to relish the food with gusto.

"Yep, all of it. Can we talk now, Preston? Really talk?"

"Sure. Why didn't you go into architecture like we talked about?" He started off with the first question.

"Because every time I looked at a drafting table I saw your face and I couldn't bear it. I was going to therapy twice a week. Daddy was ready to string me up, it wasn't doing a bit of good. He wanted me to take a year off and tour Europe just to get me away. It wasn't a good time, and . . ."

"I guess it wasn't," he said. "The ship captain had me in therapy, too. Why didn't you go to Europe?"

"I went to see Daddy over the Christmas break that year. He works for the government in a different agency than I do. Sometimes I wonder if that's why he and mother couldn't live together. They were both so smart and . . . oh, well, that's another Pandora's box to open another day. Anyway, I met Jasper at a party. It was written in the stars from there. Daddy pitched an Irishman's fit." She rolled her eyes in remembrance. "He offered me the moon to stay away from the government. He said I could name my price and he'd put the money in my bank account."

"Why? Is what you do dangerous? Just what . . ." He drew his eyebrows down in a frown.

"I could tell you, but then I'd have to kill you." She shifted her eyes toward the door and across the room as if the whole place was bugged.

"Come on, Kitty, I'm serious." He reached across the table and covered her hand with his.

"I'm a profiler for the FBI. Do you know what that means?" Her toes curled. She was glad they were tucked under the table so he couldn't see them.

"Like in the books and on the movies?" he asked.

"Not quite so glamorous," she said. "Mostly just a lot of hard brainwork and intuition. Somewhat like putting a puzzle together when the pieces are scattered. First I find the pieces and then try to make them fit into a picture."

"You're playing it down, aren't you?" He looked right into her eyes and didn't blink. "Do you carry a weapon when you're putting the puzzle together?"

She nodded.

"You ever think about cross-training into something else?"

Her temper flared and she jerked her hand away. "You wouldn't ask me to, would you?"

"Of course I would. I'd almost demand it. What you do isn't fit for a wife or a mother. What would happen if a criminal found out where you lived or that you had children? They could hurt you or your family. I couldn't let you . . ."

"You'd have no choice." She set her full mouth in a firm line. "I think we'd better talk about something else right now. My job is part of my life and I wouldn't leave it for anyone. Not even you, Preston."

"Okay." He nodded but the argument was far from over. They'd barely touched the chilly tip of the iceberg. "We'll put that one on the back burner and talk about it later."

"So what's on the agenda after supper? A moonlight walk on the beach?" She asked. He'd given in way too quickly. They'd fight on that battleground but not tonight. Not with candles and scampi and freshly kindled sparks of desire skipping around the room.

"Television movie? Listening to the quiet of the ocean waves? Miniature golf with lots of people around? Name your poison and I'll provide it," he said.

"Then I choose listening to the quiet ocean waves," she said.

"Good. I love to smell the salt and listen to the steady beat of the waves after dark," he said, shoveling more scampi in his mouth.

They finished supper and washed dishes by the flickering candlelight, neither of them quite ready to turn on the harsh overhead light. The comment she made about not changing her job for anyone, not even him, kept nagging Preston. What would he have to do to change her mind, and did he want to? He couldn't live with the everyday stress of knowing any phone call, anyone who walked through the door, might be bringing him the news that Kitty had been killed on the job. A cold knot of fear filled his chest just thinking about that scenario. It would be better to kiss her good-bye forever than live in dread the rest of his life. If he did persuade her to change her mind and she resented him for it a few months or years down the road, the relationship could go sour. He was between a rock and a hard place, and both were pinching.

"So you ready?" she asked, glad she'd opted for the beach after dark rather than a movie. Motels rooms certainly were not designed with Kitty Maguire and Preston Fleming in mind. If they had been, there would have been no sign of a bed. When she'd agreed to spend two weeks with him she hadn't thought about being in and out of bedrooms.

"Sure am." He dried his hands on the kitchen towel and jammed his room key into the pocket of his jean shorts.

"This is my beach," she said when they sat down in the still warm white sand. She drew a line between her and Preston with her finger. "This is your side. No fraternizing between the troops. You watch the stars from your side and I'll watch them from mine. We've got to talk a lot more, Preston, before we succumb to anymore of those dynamite kisses," she said.

"Sounds like you've done this before." He cocked his head and looked at her sideways.

"Are you asking or commenting?" she countered.

"Would it make a difference?"

"Hmmmm?" She twisted her mouth around. "I've spent lots of time in motels with my job. Sometimes, most times, there's a team at work. But there was no fraternizing between the troops, Preston. If that's what you're asking. Didn't you and the tall blond ever lay on the beach together?"

"Is this a test? What do I get if I pass?" He evaded the question.

"Shhhh," she said. "There was a shooting star. It means I get a wish and I have to think about it. Besides, I don't want to know about the blond. Forget I asked."

He broke the rules by reaching out across the line

drawn in the moist sand and taking her hand in his. She didn't refuse that much fraternization between the troops, but he worried about what she'd said. She didn't want to know anything about the blond. That could mean most anything, but it probably meant that she was totally indifferent to him. There she was just inches from him, lying on her back, her eyes on the stars, evidently not thinking a thing about their future.

"So what are you thinking about right now? What did you wish for on your shooting star?" he asked.

"I'm trying hard not to think of anything," she said honestly. "It's not easy with you holding my hand, but I'm trying. And I won't tell you what I wished for because it won't come true."

"I see," he said, a smile twitching at the corners of his mouth.

Kitty stared at the stars, letting a healthy dose of reality cure the infatuation she had with Preston. She wouldn't make any better wife than her mother had. She'd go into the marriage with big ideas of being Preston's wife and . . . good grief, where were those thoughts coming from anyway? Preston might have hinted that he was interested in marriage during that tirade about his wife and children and her job, but he wasn't proposing. They were on a two week vacation to get to know each other again. Maybe just to finally have closure over the fiasco Aunt Bertha had rendered.

But I still love him, she argued with herself. *At least my body does. Maybe my mind better get used to the fact that he wants something altogether different than I do out of life.* She could not . . . would not, leave her job. Preston was right. It didn't exactly go hand in hand with the society of the small town of Caddo: being a rancher's wife and raising kids. What would happen to their children when she woke up one morning and didn't want to be married after all? Did she want children? What did Kitty want. She'd better figure out pretty soon or her heart was going to overrule any common sense she might have inherited from the Mason side of the family.

"Ready for a walk?" Preston asked.

"Sure." Her voice was flat and drained. The decision wasn't going to be easy, no matter which way the chips fell.

Each in their own thoughts, each wondering what the other was thinking, they walked along in perfect silence under a lover's moon. His hand brushed hers one minute, the next her fingers were entwined with his so naturally it made her heart ache. It wasn't fair to find the perfect mate only to realize it would never work. But she and Preston were like oil and water, and the only thing produced when oil and water were mixed was one big mess.

After half an hour she reached the almighty decision.

She simply turned around and started back to the motel, her hand still clasping his firmly. She'd have this memory to hold her for all eternity. The kiss in Texas, a wonderful day on the beach, and walking barefoot in the warm sand with him. When she was an old woman like Aunt Bertha, she'd look back on this time and hope she'd made the right choice. To ignore her heart and follow what her mind knew was best for her.

"Thank you for a beautiful day," she whispered when they reached her room.

"Thank you for a beautiful day," he whispered right back as he drew her into the circle of his arms. When his lips met hers, two starving souls united. He tasted a mixture of fish, garlic, and peppermint gum she'd popped in her mouth right after supper. She didn't taste anything, just felt like she was soaring somewhere up above the clouds, as the sky lit up in a bright array of fireworks. She took a step closer and deepened the kiss. One last wonderful kiss.

He held her close for several moments after she finally pulled away from him and laid her head on his chest. It reminded him of that time when he kissed her good-bye in the front yard. The next morning he went back to the Navy. Two months later Aunt Bertha delivered her death sentence.

But it wasn't like that now. They had two weeks, minus two days, and a whole beautiful world ahead of them. With no letters to get waylaid. Nothing, not one thing could happen that the two of them together couldn't work out. Preston brushed another kiss across her forehead. "Good night, my beautiful Kitty," he said breathlessly and opened her door for her.

"Good night, Preston." She eased the door shut, and then tiptoed to watch him through the peep hole until there wasn't even a shadow left.

Chapter Thirteen

Kitty wiped away a warm, salty tear with the back of her hand as passengers loaded onto the airplane. She'd be back in Oklahoma City before daybreak. Jasper could just face the fact that she'd been gone two days and not two weeks. She'd gotten her heart and mind straightened out with one simple shrimp dinner served with candlelight flickering around in a motel room. Preston had stated his position clearly and she wasn't going to stagnate in the backwater town of Caddo, Oklahoma. So that was that! Jasper could find her a place to go. Siberia would be fine. The Sahara sounded okay. Anyplace but southern Oklahoma.

An elderly lady with purple hair took the aisle seat next to her. Whoever said today's teenagers had the market on strange-colored hair hadn't looked at pictures of their ancestors, Kitty thought. Adolescence, with all its show of rebellion, couldn't hold a backseat to the little old ladies who had been having poor results with their hair dye for years.

The woman's brilliant blue eyes twinkled in a bed of wrinkles and her mouth turned up at the corners in a smile when she saw Kitty. "Thank goodness, I've got some young company for this flight. Last leg of the journey I had to sit beside an old man who had left his hearing aid in Alaska and couldn't hear a word I said to him."

Kitty put on her fake smile. She was dealing with her last raw nerve and she didn't need a sweet, interfering grandmother, who'd no doubt tell her that she needed to stay with her job long enough to get a squad car out of the deal.

"So you on a business or pleasure trip?" the lady asked.

"Both." She cocked her head to one side, contemplating faking sleep so she could be alone with her thoughts.

"Ladies and gentlemen, we are delaying our flight for at least thirty minutes. Please feel free to sit still or go back into the airport to walk around," the captain said. Several people sighed. Kitty could have whooped and hollered.

"Well, now, why don't me and you just go find us a cup of coffee and get to know each other. By the way, my name is Clara Jones," the lady said.

"I'm so sorry," Kitty said, a hint of real, honest sorrow in her voice. "But I'm glad we've got a delay because I've really got to go to the restroom. Maybe I'll see you in the coffee shop afterwards."

"I understand, honey. When the bladder calls, a woman better be on the way with her legs crossed if she's nearing my age. I'll save you a seat in the coffee shop, just in case." Clara grinned.

Kitty spent ten minutes sitting on a bench in the powder room part of the bathroom. She counted the holes in a ceiling block, committed that number to memory. Twelve blocks down, ten across. One hundred and twenty blocks, multiplied by the number of holes. She was playing head games to make the time go faster. Anything to get past the next twenty minutes. Past . . . did that word actually flutter through her mind? Had there ever been a ray of hope from the past for her and Preston, or was this two week thing just reverse psychology on Jasper's part? Send her down there for a couple of weeks and she'll get so bored she'll be crazy. Was she right in listening to common sense? Looking toward the future and being sensible? Or should she listen to the vibes coming straight from the heart, call a cab, and hightail it back to the hotel? And hope when she got back to the hotel, he was still there and he hadn't found the note?

I'm confused, Kitty admitted to herself. *I thought I had it all figured out at the hotel and that this was the right thing to do. Now my heart is hurting and I think I've made the biggest mistake of my life. Maybe I ought to go back and fight it out with him. Not lay around on the beach holding hands, or kissing goodnight at the door. But just lay my cards on the table and let him put his there, too.*

Disagreeable vibes bounced around inside Kitty like they were doing a rain dance. Thinking of a lifetime with Preston was enough to about make her knees weak. But would she get bored with the ranch in a month, or six months, or six years, and then hate him? She couldn't take that chance. Not for her sake, or his.

What seemed like the only answer a couple of hours before now wasn't right. She could feel something coming straight from the heart. Strange, that fate had sent a little blue-haired lady to make her hide out in a private place and a thirty-minute delay to question her decision to go back home to Oklahoma City. She frowned as she walked down the concourse toward the bank of telephones.

Timothy Maguire's booming voice filled her ears a few minutes later. It sounded a bit hoarse, like he'd been asleep. "Daddy?" she said. "Were you napping?"

"No, I was sound asleep. It happens to be four o'clock in the morning, Kitty. Most people aren't napping at this time of night. Now tell me what's so wrong that you're calling me in the middle of the night," he said.

"Daddy, I'm in Florida with Preston Fleming. At least I was with him. I'm at the airport because I'm leaving him, but I think I've changed my mind. I'm more confused than I've ever been. I've listened to my good sense and it told me to go back to Oklahoma and my job. That was the important thing in my life. Now I feel like I should've listened to my heart. It's telling me one thing and good sense is telling me another. Suddenly, I needed a bit of advice. You're an Irishman and you always listen to your heart, yet look what happened when you did. You and Mother didn't make it."

"I didn't listen to my stubborn Irish heart," Timothy said. "I told it to shut up and with the obstinate Irish blood flowing in my veins, I went right ahead with what I wanted and forgot about my heart's warnings. I wanted your mother to be my wife and my heart told me it would never work. She didn't want to get married. Had her life mapped out all the way to the day she was ninety years old. But I was determined to make her into what I wanted her to be. I kept begging until she said yes. Then she didn't want children and I nagged until we had you. If I had listened to my heart I would have never married her, just kept company with her the rest of our days. But then I wouldn't have had you, and you have always been the light of my life."

"But," Kitty was more confused than ever. "Why did you let Aunt Bertha have me?"

"Because I could never tell your mother no. I was traveling all over the world by the time she told me she was finished with our marriage. Then a few years later she called and told me she only had a few months to live. I thought my heart was going to stop beating. I'd always figured I could use my Irish charm and make her change her mind and come back to me. Then she was gone. Just like that, Kitty. My Katherine was gone. You were twelve years old and needed a stable life, and Katherine wanted you to go to school where she had, in Caddo. I was heartbroken, but my career kept me traveling all over the world, so it was boarding school or Caddo for you. She wanted you to live in Caddo, and I couldn't refuse her a single thing, anyway. I figured you'd ask these questions, my child, but not in the middle of the night all these years later."

"Daddy, my heart says it loves Preston Fleming. Common sense says go home and forget him. I want to listen to my heart, but I'm scared it's just reaching out for something it once had, and everything has changed since then," she said.

"That's your battlefield, Kitty Maguire. Five years ago you called me and told me you were in love with the young man. You seemed more sure of yourself then than you are now. It's the same young man and you've got the same heart."

"Things have changed," she said, wondering the whole time if she was trying to convince her father or herself.

"All I can tell you is to listen to your heart, and I think down deep you've already figured that out. You just need a little reassurance, which is pretty natural considering the upbringing you had from Aunt Bertha. But if you decide to listen to good sense instead, then go home. Jasper said he'd sent you away for a couple of weeks because you weren't fit for the field. If you've truly made up your mind to stay with the job, then get back into it. It can be the love of your life. It doesn't offer much warmth on cold winter nights, but it'll fill your days with something profitable to get you from daylight to dark. You've loved Preston Fleming for years. It doesn't mean you can live with him, but can you live without him? Be honest with yourself. I'm going back to sleep. Call me at a decent hour when you make up your mind. Good-bye, Kitty."

"Thanks, Daddy," she said.

She headed back toward the airplane. She couldn't live with him. She'd proved that in less than forty-eight hours. Passion was the only glue holding the relationship together. When that was gone, she'd resent him for sure. She'd managed to live without him for five years, so she could do it another five or ten or fifty.

She stopped at the front of the plane long enough to ask the flight attendant if she could take a seat at the back instead of where she'd been assigned. The woman agreed, since the red eye flight was only half full. Clara was already busy visiting with another blue-haired lady by the time the plane was in the sky. Kitty unbuckled the belt, drew her knees up next to her chest, and buried her face in them. She was more miserable than she'd been her entire life, including the day Aunt Bertha had lied. By the time she reached Oklahoma City, she'd figured she had just ruined her life, and there wasn't a thing she could do to change it.

Preston awoke in a cold sweat at exactly four o'clock. He must have been dreaming, but he couldn't remember anything that had happened to make him feel so empty and sad. He fluffed up his pillow, but when he buried his head in it he caught the faint lingering aroma of Kitty's perfume. A vision came to him of her hugging the pillow as she waited for him to put his shoes on before they went to the beach. He crawled out of bed, made coffee, and took a cup out to the balcony. No light showed around the drapes in her room, so she must still be sleeping. Just like he should have been.

At five o'clock he poured a second cup of coffee for himself and one for Kitty. He'd wake her and they'd watch the sun come up from the beach. He set the mugs on the table between a couple of lawn chairs and knocked on the door. No answer. She must have been really tired the night before. All he had to do was crack open the door at the motel in Dallas and she was off the bed like a shot. A few hours of relaxation and all those finely tuned instincts had flown right out the window. In two weeks she'd have a whole new lease on life. He knocked again. Still no answer. He went back into his room and dialed her room number and waited while it rang twenty times.

Then he began to worry.

He went back into his room and picked up the extra plastic room key she'd handed him when they checked into the motel. "In case I get locked out," she said. "Give me your extra one and then maybe we won't have to come back to the office when we can't get in."

He held his breath for a moment when he opened the door. What if some lunatic had recognized her and she was dead? The job. The one she wouldn't give up for anyone may have taken her from him just at the moment when everything was going right. The bed was rumpled but unslept in. Everything was gone. No baggage. No Kitty.

A note was propped up on the pillow.

" 'My dearest Preston'," he read aloud. " 'I can't do it. Life led us on different roads and they can never mesh together. You said if I had doubts or changed my mind I could go home, no questions asked. I'm going home. Kitty'."

His heart stopped beating just like it had that day in Trinidad.

Chapter Fourteen

Oranges, pinks, yellows, and pure white combined forces to provide Preston with a beautiful sunset. He watched in solemn silence as the orange ball dipped behind the tree limbs. The ice cubes melted in his glass of tea, watering it down to a faint amber color. A grasshopper helped itself to a drink from the condensation on the side of the dewy glass and Preston didn't even shoo it away.

Nothing made a bit of sense. He'd gone over every single word he'd said, every moment they'd shared. The kisses, the lingering looks. All of it and nothing should have made her bolt like a jackrabbit. Not one single thing. Except that comment he'd made about her job. He heard the crunch of gravel in the driveway. One of his brothers coming to feed the stock, probably. He sighed. That's all he needed to cap off a horrid day. To have to explain why he was sitting on his deck

169

when he should have been cuddled up next to Kitty Maguire on the beach.

"Hello," Kitty said cautiously and slid into the chaise lounge beside him.

Without moving his head, he cut his eyes around to look at her. Who did she think she was anyway? To rip his heart out by the roots, stomp on it until it resembled a cow patty, and toss it by the wayside for the buzzards to feed on. Then appear on his deck like the Queen-of-blasted-Sheba and sit down beside him. Well, there would be a blizzard at high noon tomorrow on Main Street in Caddo before he ever gave her another chance to inflict that kind of pain on him again.

"I'm sorry." She bit her quivering lip. "I made a mistake."

He looked back at the last dregs of the sunset. The stars were already taking up their places in the sky around a big round lover's moon. Lovers. Something they'd never be because Kitty Maguire had wallowed around in Bertha Mason's gene pool too long. She hated men. Or was it just Preston Fleming who raised her ire to the boiling point?

"What do I have to do?" She grabbed his arm and wished she hadn't when the shock shook her insides like a tornado ripping up a house. She set her full mouth in a tight, firm line and willed him to look at her. He didn't. "I made a mistake. I admit it. Do you expect me to get down on my knees and beg? Well, I won't, Preston Fleming. If you can't at least turn your head around and look at me, then I'll get back in my truck and go home. I drove down here to tell you I made a colossal mistake. I should have fought it out with you rather than running away. But I don't know jack about relationships. I come from a dysfunctional family of the first degree. Aunt Bertha hated men in general. My mother was a career person. My father, bless his heart, told me to follow my heart, but I'm scared he might even be wrong, Preston. Am I going to be like my mother and walk out on you in five years? Am I going to be like Aunt Bertha and hate you somewhere down the line? It scares the devil out of me just thinking about it. I've never been around a baby in my life, unless you count kittens and puppies. I'm not a very good cook, but I can clean house. Aunt Bertha saw to that. I love you so much it hurts, but I'm scared out of my mind. You're not helping one blessed bit, sitting there in all your pouting condemnation."

"I. Am. Not. Pouting."

"Yes you are, and righteously so. If the situation were reversed I'd probably tell you to take your fanny right back to Oklahoma City." She withdrew her hand from his arm. The warmth remaining in her fingertips was enough to set her whole arm on fire.

"Why?" he asked.

"Because you said that about my job. It was my security blanket. It's been . . . how do I tell you, Preston? You were gone. My heart was shattered so badly I didn't think it would ever be in one piece again. Aunt Bertha was dead. What little stability I'd had was shot to the moon. Daddy was somewhere in a third world country. Then the job came along. I studied for it. Day and night. It became my obsession. Learn. Study. Do the work for the job. Finally I was in the field doing what I was trained for, what apparently was my niche in real life. Making money even though I didn't need it. Kitty, carving out a place in a tough world and doing a fine job of it. To leave it would mean to . . ." She stopped.

His face was as blank as a sheet of paper. He really didn't understand. She had parked her truck in the front yard and knocked lightly on the door. When he didn't answer she had simply walked around back, thinking that she might sit on the deck and wait until he came back from wherever he had been. When she realized he was sitting there quietly she thought she'd faint. Her knees were limp strands of overcooked spaghetti but she made them carry her up the two steps and sit down beside him. He wasn't wearing a shirt, and the soft bed of black hair on his chest made her gasp. She wanted to snuggle up beside him on the cushiony lounge and rest her check in all that hair, but she didn't dare tempt fate that far. And the look on his face said he flat didn't care what she had to say, not even the admission that she loved him with every fiber of her being.

Preston stood up without saying a word. She expected him to go inside the house and lock the door behind himself. It was what she fully well deserved. Tears formed down deep in her soul but she resolutely kept them from making the journey to her eyes. She'd take her broken pride and crushed dignity back to her apartment. She'd prayed for an answer when she was above the clouds in the airplane on the way to Oklahoma City. When she opened the door to her empty apartment she thought she had the message straight from her heart. *Go to Caddo. If he's there, tell him just how you feel. Be honest and it will all work out.*

Preston sat down on the edge of her lounge and eased her over with his long, muscular body. He slipped one arm under her and used the other one to draw her so close that her cheek nestled in the hair on his chest. She could hear his heart beating steadily, rhythmically, and it lulled her into a peaceful state she had felt in his house a few days before.

"Trust me," he whispered into her hair.

"I'm afraid." Her voice quivered just slightly.

"Don't tell me you're afraid." He almost chuckled.

"Of life. Not of the job. I can do the job and I'm good at it. Life and love both scare the liver out of me, Preston." If only she could stay wrapped in his arms forever. But "if only" didn't happen in real life.

"Then do your job and come home to me when it's done every time. I can live with it if I have to, Kitty. Just don't be satisfied with the job and make it your whole life. I want you. But if I can only have what's left after the job, I'll take that and be happy to get it. Just don't ever leave me again with nothing but an empty heart. I can't bear it. I thought when your Aunt Bertha told me that lie I'd never know love again. Never have that special feeling I had with you. Never feel . . . there's no words to describe it, are there? That I'd never feel that way again. We've been given a second chance in a world where second chances are miracles. If you have to work, then I'll live with that decision because I love you so much. Just leave some-thing for me when you come in the front door, darlin'." He cleared the lump from his throat. "Because what I ask is that the part of your heart that I get is mine and mine alone. I don't want to share what time you give me with anyone or anything."

His heart skipped a beat while he waited.

Her chin quivered. Unconditional love. He'd just offered her the world on a silver platter and the moon and stars for dessert. "Thank you," she murmured and raised her eyes to find him staring down at her with so much love and passion it literally took her breath away. Somewhere in the middle of his speech he'd said something that gripped her heart. *Because I love you so much.* That's why he didn't want her to work for the agency. Not because he had a problem with a wife working but because of fear he would lose her.

"There's something else I better tell you. I went by the office today and told Jasper . . ." she paused. "It's a long story. I didn't know if you would toss me out on my ear or even if you would be here. You might have still been in Florida. After all, it's your two week vacation. But if you . . ." she stammered and swallowed hard.

"Spit it out, Kitty. I'm here. We've said our piece to each other." He gently rubbed circles on the back of her bare arm. The sensation of having her so near when he had thought it was completely over was like water to a man dying of thirst. If she only came home a few nights a month and brought him this kind of bliss, he could survive.

"I told Jasper if things worked out for us, I couldn't work at the agency. The last case was very difficult. I kept seeing your face and I couldn't concentrate," she admitted.

He grinned. "So you thought about me and had trouble doing your job. Does that make me powerful or what?"

"Hush," she snapped and tried to roll away from him, but his strong muscular arms kept her close. A song went through her mind. Strange as it might seem, that too was a message from her heart. It was an old country tune. The words said something about the day the singer started loving a person again. It mentioned being right back where they'd really always been. She was where she should have been all those years. In Preston's arms and in his life.

"Are we going back to Florida then?" He tightened his hold on her.

"No, we are not. We are going to stay right here in Caddo. I feel peaceful in this house. It's the only place I've felt that since I was a little girl and I'm not leaving it," she declared.

"Is that a proposal? Are you going to marry me to get the house?"

"I'm going to marry you to get you," she said. "Tomorrow morning I talk to the president at Southeastern Oklahoma State University in Durant. If he hires me, and Jasper thinks he will stand on his head in hot ashes to get me, then I start teaching in the Criminology department in three weeks. Can you live with that?"

He sat straight up, nearly toppling her off in the floor with the sudden motion. "You really aren't going back to the agency? Are you serious? Are we really going to get married? I mean, this is serious, will you marry me?"

She giggled. "No, I'm not going back to the agency. I've turned in a resignation contingent upon us working out our problems. I have to work because I'll go crazy if I don't. The job is only for a year. Someone is on sabbatical. I'm very serious, and yes, we're going to get married. You asked me five years ago to marry you and I said yes then. The answer hasn't changed. The two kids who were so much in love have changed, somewhat. But I think we can adjust the program for the differences."

"When?" He sighed deeply. If anyone ever told him there were no miracles in today's haphazard, give-me world he would disagree with them entirely.

"Well, you've still got twelve days of your vacation left and I've got three weeks until I go to work if I get hired. Tomorrow morning I interview. How about tomorrow afternoon? We could jump over the line into Texas and come home married," she suggested.

"But the family will want to be there," he protested and moaned at the same time.

"The family can give us a huge reception at the church," she said. "We'll even repeat our vows before the priest if they want us to. They can do it up right. Daddy can even fly in for the hoopla, but I'm not waiting two months or even two weeks to be your wife, Preston. I've waited five years. That's long enough. And besides, I'm tired of listening to common sense and my mind. I'm listening to my heart and hoping it isn't leading me down the wrong path."

"I promise it's not. You don't want the white dress and . . ." He could scarcely believe his ears.

"I want you. I swallowed my pride and apologized. I walked what seemed like twenty miles from my truck to this back porch. I made myself sit down beside you when I was scared out of my mind you'd tell me to go home. I don't want to be engaged, Preston. I want to be married to you. I want to wake up with you next to me in that big four-poster bed back there in your bedroom." She shifted her weight slightly and sat in his lap. She pulled his face down to hers. "I think most people seal their engagement with a kiss like this," she whispered. Behind their closed eyes, the skies lit up in an array of beautiful colors.

Chapter Fifteen

Kitty stepped into the dress she'd chosen for the reception. A watered silk the color of a shiny new dime with a billowy skirt and tight-fitting bodice. She planned to walk into the church on Preston's arm, so she didn't need a bouquet. She fastened the chain with the little open heart ring dangling on it around her neck. "Thank you for keeping it for me, Bear," she said softly. She scattered a few fresh daisies in her upswept chestnut hair. Last week she'd married Preston in a civil ceremony. He'd worn his starched jeans and a white western shirt and she'd worn a plain white silk dress with a corsage of white roses.

She'd had her way then. A wedding with just the two of them, and a whole week of wondrous honeymoon following. The thrill of snuggling up to him in the four-poster bed and waking up in his arms with the sun spraying warmth into their bedroom. Enjoying breakfast together and walking hand in hand over every square inch of the ranch. Today was for her father and the Fleming family. She'd been a bride, now she'd be a Irish wife in her rustling silk dress.

Preston opened the bedroom door and whistled in appreciation. "My oh my, but I do believe I like you as well in that as in that pretty white dress you wore to our real wedding."

"My darlin'." She tiptoed to kiss his mouth. "I was a pure bride then. Today I'm an Irish wife, and nobody better ever mess with my marriage. I might be tempted to use my Irish blood and put a curse upon their sorry hides."

"I love you, Kitty." He kissed her passionately and walked her backwards until she felt the edge of the bed on the back of her legs.

"Oh, no, you don't," she giggled. "I'm already dressed and we're to be at the church in exactly twenty minutes. I'll have to drive to get us there on time now."

"No, you won't drive. You've got to keep that lead foot off the gas pedal, Kitty. I'll drive," he said. "It won't matter if we are a few minutes late. They sure won't have the wedding without us. Twice married. Does that mean it'll take two divorces to untangle us?"

"That means you better never use that word again in my presence." She cocked her head to one side. "I won't have a daughter grow up like I did. We'll stay together forever and love each other three days past that."

"Daughter? I tell you the firstborn is always a boy in the Fleming family," he teased.

"And I tell you we need a daughter first so she can

take care of her brothers like your sisters did you when you were little. But I won't say a word if we start out our family with twin sons, Preston. Not a word. Even though I don't know a thing about babies, I want a house full of them. If I don't know what to do, I'll call one of your sisters. Thinking about being a mother fills my heart and soul with joy. Now let's go get married. In the church so our parents won't worry about it coming undone."

The priest heard their sacred vows said before the immediate family. Preston slipped the plain gold band on his wife's finger and repeated solemnly to love, cherish, and honor her until death. The words didn't have to be repeated. They were already engraved upon his heart forever . . . not just until death. For theirs was a union made in heaven, not simply on earth. Kitty slipped the matching gold wedding ring on his finger and repeated her vows. Today was supposed to have been five years before, but she'd forgiven Aunt Bertha. A heart that holds grudges and hatred has no room for love to grow, and there would be only love begotten from her heart.

"And now to the reception," Alan said when the traditional kiss was finished. The reception hall was overflowing with guests and food. They stood in the receiving line for what seemed like hours. Everyone in all of Bryan County it appeared had come to wish them a long and happy life together. Kitty's smile was getting tired toward the end of the line when she looked up to see her old friend, Lisa, standing before her.

"I'm so sorry." Lisa stumbled over the words and wiped away tears. "If only I'd answered your letter or called, we could have straightened all this out together."

"Let's forget it." Kitty opened her arms and hugged Lisa tightly. "Bring the children to see me next week. Preston tells me you have two now. I have a whole week when Preston will be at work and before my job at the college begins. We've wasted too much time as it is. I need to get to know your girls. Is the next one a boy?"

Lisa patted her rounded stomach. "I hope so. If it's a third girl, then Jody will just have to make the last one a football player because three is the limit," she laughed. "I'll call on Monday."

"Thank you for putting the light back in Kitty's eyes," Timothy said when he shook hands with his new son-in-law. He really liked the young man. Too bad things had happened the way they did, but thank goodness it had all been rectified.

"She's put the light back in mine, too," Preston said. "Come see us at the ranch anytime."

"I'll do it," he promised with a wink.

"Can I call you when I get a really tough case?" Jasper was the last one in line to hug Kitty.

"I don't think it would work. I'm so happy it's unreal, Jasper," she said, patting his shoulder.

"I didn't think you'd stay down here in this place," he sighed.

"Hey, you're the one who sent me, remember," she teased. "Come see us when the going gets too tough in Oklahoma City. We'll pamper you and spoil you rotten. You might even resign your position and start a hog farm."

He just shook his head and moved on.

After cutting the huge wedding cake, the band began to play a slow waltz, and Preston led Kitty to the floor for the first dance. He hummed into her hair as they swayed to the music.

"Aren't you glad we went to Texas now?" She tilted her head back and looked up at him. Preston Fleming was hers at long last. His smile was hers and the kiss he bent to give her—most definitely was hers alone. And like she'd found out for herself after she left him in a Florida motel room, anything worth having was worth fighting for. Be it man, woman, or even Kitty, herself. She'd fought a legion of devils coming back to Caddo, tearing up her own comfortable rut. But in the end she'd listened to her heart, and it was sure beginning to look like it knew what would make her happy. Every other battle paled in comparison to that war she fought on the plane from Florida to Oklahoma.

"Yes, I'm glad we didn't wait," he answered. "I would have been a raving lunatic by now. Instead, we can enjoy this wonderful reception."

"Does that mean we have to stay until the last dog's dead? I'd rather be at home with you," she whispered so softly only he heard it.

"Honeymoon is over, darlin'. We have to stay," he declared.

"We may have to stay but the honeymoon won't ever be over. Not ever. Not even when I'm old and wrinkled. When my hair is gray and I'm using a cane,

I'll still want to be with you." High color filled her cheeks when she spoke.

"Is that a promise?" He remembered the empty feeling in his heart when he'd walked into the motel room and found her gone. "You'll never leave me again? I'll never find a note on the pillow?"

She read his mind. "Never. Hold me close, Preston."

"Yes, ma'am." He hugged her even tighter. "Your dad seems to be getting along right well with Nora." He nodded toward Timothy and one of the ladies from the church.

"Hmmm." Kitty laid her head back on his chest and shut her eyes. She'd made the right decisions. There wasn't anything behind her eyelids but contentment and peace.

The two step ended and her father was at her elbow. "I think it's the proper thing now for the father of the grand and beautiful bride to dance with her. And you, my son, are supposed to dance with your lovely mother," he said.

"Yes, sir." Preston put Kitty's hand in her father's and went in search of his mother, like tradition demanded.

"Well, my child, I'm glad that you listened to your heart. I like the young man and his family. It'll do you good to have a big, nurturing family around you. I'll worry about you a lot less in the days to come," Timothy said as they danced a true Irish waltz to the music he'd asked for, "Ramblin' Irishman." He sang the words as he dipped and swayed her in proper Irish style.

"Daddy," she said. "It's been a long time since

Momma died. If you wanted to . . . well, if there would be another woman . . . I wouldn't . . ."

"Kitty!" A grin covered his whole handsome face. "I had a perfect love once. She was everything I wanted even if I wasn't everything she wanted. My Katherine was," he said slowly, his green eyes soft with a faraway expression and his voice hoarse from just speaking her name. "She wouldn't have liked this day. You giving up your job and moving to Caddo. But I love it, my child. Your Irish has finally surfaced. But my Katherine." He cleared his throat and searched for the words while Kitty waited. Timothy Maguire speechless was a rare thing. "She filled me with happiness," he finally said. "I don't need another woman like that again. Katherine was a breath of spring combined with the heat of summer. I love her still and will forever. When this life is over she'll be waiting for me on the other side where the hills are as green as an Irish countryside and the sunsets are beautiful. Thank you, Kitty, for your fine offer, but you'll have to make do with one old Daddy who falls in and out of Oklahoma randomly. Give me grandchildren to fill my life and I'll be a happy old man."

"You'll never be old," she snorted. "I love you, Daddy."

The music changed with barely a second's intermission into "Scarce O'Tatties," a short, snappy, true Irish reel. Kitty stepped back from Timothy, picked up the flowing skirt of her long, silk dress, and with a sharp click of her heels, they locked their arms at the elbow and executed a circling fast dance like no one in the room had ever seen.

"Ah, my child," he panted when the ninety seconds of music finished. "You have not forgotten your Irish upbringing or the way to a father's heart."

Kitty kissed him on the forehead and laughed. "And I never will. You must come and show your grand-daughter the reel when she learns to walk."

"Granddaughter? Already?" He raised a heavy red eyebrow.

"Not that I know of, but I want a daughter so badly, Daddy. Of course I want sons, too. A big old rambling family like the Flemings. To take care of each other through the good times and the bad," she said.

"A daughter with your temper?" he teased.

"Probably, but we'll teach her when she's very young to listen to her heart and we'll shoot anyone who messes with her life or her mail," she laughed again. "Daddy, I've forgiven Aunt Bertha. My heart can't harbor hate when there's love to be had."

"You truly are Irish. I'm glad you have forgiven the lady. She was a picture of what happens when hate controls the heart. I wouldn't want that for my daughter. Forgiveness is good." Timothy kissed her forehead. "Now go do your duty by that fine young man. Make him happy and he'll do the same for you."

Preston stood on the sidelines and said a silent prayer of thanksgiving. To see Kitty's eyes twinkle again made his heart swell with joy. To know that she truly belonged to him forever was almost more than he could believe. She held out her hand to him on the next song, a fast Irish reel, and he just shook his head. She crossed the room, laced her fingers in his, and led him to the middle of the floor amid an applauding audience.

"Just stand still, my darlin', I shall do the work on this one," she said so quietly no one heard it except the groom. "Cross your arms over your chest and pretend to be mad at me. Kind of like you were when I walked up on the porch last week. When you just cut your eyes around and wouldn't even look at me. I shall give you a dose of my Irish blood and dance away the anger."

Preston almost blushed but he did what she said. He crossed his arms across his chest and she proceeded to twist and twirl around him, touching his shoulder seductively at one moment, brushing a kiss across his mouth, and flirting blatantly in front of everyone. When the song finished she uncrossed his arms, put them around her waist and stepped inside the circle so close to him that he could feel her pounding heart. She laced her fingers behind his neck. "Kiss me, Preston. The fight is over and we are now ready to face the world. Never fear, my darling. We shall feel that way again everyday for the rest of this life and the one beyond the last breath we take in this world."

"Yes, ma'am." His big blue eyes never left hers for a second. As far as Kitty and Preston were concerned, there was no one else in the room.

Just Preston and Kitty Fleming as they promised each other with a kiss before a room full of witnesses that they would always feel that way again . . . forever.